The MYSTERY of the

The **MYSTERY** of the

MARTY CHAN

thistledown press

Thistledown Press Ltd.
118 - 20th Street West
Saskatoon, Saskatchewan, S7M 0W6
www.thistledownpress.com

Library and Archives Canada Cataloguing in Publication

Chan, Marty
The mystery of the cyber bully / Marty Chan.
(Marty Chan mystery series ; 4)
ISBN 978-1-897235-82-9
I. Title. II. Series.
PS8555.H39244M978 2010   jC813'.54   C2010-905544-6

Cover illustration by Laura Lee Osborne
Cover and book design by Jackie Forrie
Printed and bound in Canada

 Canada Council Conseil des Arts
for the Arts du Canada
 SASKATCHEWAN ARTS BOARD
 Canadian Patrimoine
Heritage canadien

We acknowledge the support of the Canada Council for the Arts, the Saskatchewan
Arts Board, and the Government of Canada through the Canada Book Fund for
our publishing program.

ACKNOWLEDGEMENTS

Wei Wong, Michelle Chan, Laura Lee Osborne, Jackie Forrie, R.P. MacIntyre, Mayfield Elementary School.

CHAPTER ONE

Guilty people have a certain look.

The most obvious sign was a shiny forehead. Sweat was a poor detective's lie-detector test; where there was perspiration, there was always criminal motivation. If the suspect was doing the got-to-pee shuffle, she was probably guilty. No one other than shoplifters and two-year-olds who drank too much apple juice did that two-step dance. The surefire sign of guilt? Zigzag eyes.

Walking the beat in my parents' grocery store, I'd seen it all. Last year, I caught a teenager stuffing a car magazine down his pants, and I stood back as the red-faced boy tried to explain the bulge in his pants to Mom. Last month, the shifty gaze of a teenage girl gave her away. I found two chocolate bars under her Bedazzled jean jacket, and she tried to convince Dad that she had bought them at a convenience store, but burst into hiccup tears when he asked her to show him the receipt. Today, I was sure I was staring at the sweaty forehead of another thief.

The raven wing of hair dangling in front of Samantha McNally's pale face couldn't hide the bead of perspiration rolling down her cheek, and her heavy black eyeliner couldn't mask her shifty gaze. I was sure my grade six classmate was looking for a five-finger discount as I watched her tug the bottom of her black T-shirt and stretch out the silk-screened emo teddy bear.

She stopped when she noticed me eyeing her hands. "Um . . . I'm looking for . . . uh . . . shampoo. Where is it?" she asked.

Silence melted a shoplifter's nerve like a hair dryer blowing on a soft-serve ice cream cone. All I had to do was keep quiet and watch Samantha's resolve dissolve into a milky puddle of excuses to be anywhere but here. She wiped her moist forehead with her wide, black wristband and shuffled from one foot to the other, but she steeled her nerve and asked, "Are you going to tell me or not?"

This shoplifter was a tough one. "Third aisle, halfway down. Follow the smell of lilacs."

She turned on her heels and walked away. As soon as she rounded the corner, I fished out a black and silver walkie-talkie from my pocket and pressed the talk button. "Alpha One to Alpha Two," I said. "Do you read? Over."

I released the button and waited for an answer.

Static blasted out of the speaker followed by a boy's voice. "Alpa . . . erk . . . Ober."

"Say again, Alpha Two. Over."

"Werk jer yu bay? Ober."

"Remi, can you hear me? Over."

Now only static burst from my walkie-talkie's silver speaker.

I pushed the talk button. "Say again," I said. "Over."

My walkie-talkie was half of an ancient set that belonged to my best friend Remi Boudreau. He claimed they were weapons in the war on crime, but mine was jamming and I didn't have time to fix it. I glanced at the large security mirror hanging at the back of the store. Reflected in the shiny fish eyeball glass, Samantha reached for something on the shelf. My body tensed ready to spring into action, but she stepped back and glanced at Mrs. Johnson who rolled her shopping cart to a stop beside her. Samantha wouldn't try anything as long as there was a witness — shoplifters were cockroaches who skittered away when people came near — and Mrs. Johnson wasn't going anywhere soon. She always read the nutrition labels to find the healthiest food. She constantly harassed my dad about the food he stocked in the store, claiming he'd get more customers if his groceries had low sodium, low fat, and low sugar. Her son Eric complained her cooking had low flavour, which was probably why he was always stealing lunches from grade three kids.

As Mrs. Johnson read a can of tomato sauce, I pressed the walkie-talkie button and whispered, "Alpha Two, come back to rendezvous point. Hurry. Over."

"Pull the antenna up and you'll get better reception," Remi said, his voice now sounding crystal clear.

"Don't need to. The problem's fixed," I said into the walkie-talkie. "It sounds like you're next to me. Over."

"That's because I am," he said.

I spun around. Remi held his walkie-talkie in one hand. Through his long brown bangs, I could see the frustration in his brown eyes. He pointed at the extended antenna on his walkie-talkie.

"No time to worry about that," I said. "Goldilocks is in the bear's house."

"Really?" he said, brightening. He scanned the store as he rolled up the sleeves of his Toronto Maple Leafs hockey jersey. "Where?"

"Momma Bear's chair," I replied.

"Which aisle is that again?" he asked.

"Salon supplies . . . shampoo . . . moisturizers . . . far right," I said.

"Couldn't you say far right in the first place? Your code is confusing, Marty."

"It's simple, Remi. Goldilocks is the one who ate the bears' porridge."

"So that means you're Momma Bear." He grinned.

"No, yes. Never mind," I said. "You got your badge?"

"Yup," he said. He reached into his back pocket and pulled out a cardboard star that read, "Remi Boudreau, Store Detective."

"Keep it close. You might need it if things get ugly."

Remi cocked his head to the side. "Ugly? How?"

"This one looks like a runner," I explained. "The badge should stop her."

He practiced flashing his badge. "'Hey, you. Yeah, I'm talking to you. You better believe I'm talking to you. You deaf or something? I said I'm talking to you. Put your hands behind your head.' How's that, Marty?"

"You got the hang of it. Now head to the far end of the aisle and keep your eyes on Goldilocks. I'll watch from this end. Right now, all we do is watch. Don't do anything until she starts to eat the porridge."

"Sure thing, Momma Bear," Remi said.

"Alpha One," I corrected.

"Sure thing," he said. "Momma Bear." He flashed me a goofy grin.

I shook my head. "Get going," I said, "Baby Bear."

He smacked my arm and jogged down the middle aisle to get into position. I looked back at the security mirror. Mrs. Johnson was still reading the label on the can of tomatoes. A few feet away, Samantha picked up a small bottle. Too small to be shampoo. I crept to the end of the aisle to get a closer look.

Samantha held a bottle of pink nail polish. The bottle was one of the oldest items in the store. Dad said the dust on the bottle was probably older than me, but he refused to stock any new bottles until this one was sold. Bright pink nail polish was an odd choice for a girl who was constantly painting her fingernails black. She placed the bottle back on the shelf, jammed her right hand in her pants pocket, pulled out her hand, and grabbed the bottle again. I inched forward. Samantha flicked her head in my direction. I jumped back around the corner, pulled out my walkie-talkie, extended the antenna and pressed the talk button.

"Alpha Two, my position has been compromised. Put your eyes on Goldilocks. Over."

"Eyes on Goldilocks. Got it. Over."

No matter what went down, I knew I could count on Remi. As the top hockey player on the Bouvier Bobcats, he was the most popular kid in town. Everyone wanted to hang out with him, but he'd rather spend time with me. When his teammates made fun of the thick lenses of my new glasses, he stood up for me and told them he'd use their noggins for slapshot practice if they didn't shut up. I knew he'd always have my back and I'd always have his.

In the security mirror, Samantha fidgeted as if she were standing on hot coals. She hadn't made her move yet, but soon. She kept picking up the bottle and putting it back on the shelf, and I started to wonder if she was going to try to make her move with Mrs. Johnson behind her. Suddenly, Remi entered the reflection.

He lifted his cardboard badge and announced, "Store detective. Freeze! You're busted."

I scrambled to back up my partner, but Remi wasn't aiming his badge at Samantha. He was staring at a very irate Mrs. Johnson.

The sharp-nosed woman huffed, "I don't have time for your childish games."

"Save it for the police, ma'am. Marty, Goldilocks ate the porridge."

I rushed to my friend's side, slipping past Samantha.

"What are you doing?" I asked Remi.

"She put something in her purse," he said.

"I told you to watch out for Goldilocks."

He pointed at the blonde-haired Mrs. Johnson. "I am."

"Not her," I said. "Her!" I pointed back down the aisle, but Samantha was gone.

"I demand an apology," Mrs. Johnson said, her shrill voice rising higher and louder like an opera singer. Any higher and she'd shatter the glass in the security mirror.

"What did you see, Remi?" I asked.

He pointed at Mrs. Johnson's purse. "She ripped a piece of paper from one of the cans and slipped it in there."

"Which can?" I asked.

Remi pointed at the cans of corn. All but one can had a coupon attached to the front. The coupon gave the shopper a discount on a can of tomatoes; the same can sitting in Mrs. Johnson's cart.

Mrs. Johnson glared at him. "I could easily shop at the IGA if this is the treatment I'm going to get here," she threatened.

Every Saturday, she bought enough groceries to make up for our lack of business during the rest of the week. She was our family's life preserver. Without her, my parents' store would sink like a lead weight. We couldn't afford to lose her business even if Remi was right, but still he was my partner.

"I want to talk to your father, Marty."

"You have to buy the corn to get the coupon," I said.

Remi looked up from her purse. "Actually, I was wrong about the coupon. I should have been asking you about the stolen grapes."

"What grapes?" she huffed.

He nodded at her purse. Inside, I could make out a barren grape stem. I grinned at my sharp-eyed partner.

"Then why do you keep that grape stem in your purse?" I asked.

Mrs. Johnson snapped her purse shut. Her gaze zigzagged and I thought I saw a bead of sweat on her temple as she did the got-to-pee shuffle. "What's in my purse is my own business, but if you're such a stickler for rules, I'll buy the can of corn."

She reached for a can on the shelf.

"No, Mrs. Johnson. You should buy the one that you took the coupon from," Remi said.

She glared at him. "I was getting two cans."

She also picked up the can with the missing coupon and placed both in her cart. Remi beamed. I turned back to where Samantha had been. Not only was she gone, so was the nail polish.

"Follow me," I ordered. "Hurry!"

We skidded to a stop by the cash register where my dad was bagging Samantha's purchases. His fingertips were blackened with the ink from the Chinese newspaper he was reading. Even his gold-rimmed glasses were smudged with ink. He had plenty of time to read, because we had so few customers. His dirty hands left fingerprints all over the plastic bag, which he handed to Samantha. She smiled at him, flashed me a dirty look and walked out.

"Dad, what did she buy?" I asked.

"Why are you not working?" he asked, fixing us a look over his gold-rimmed glasses.

"We think that girl stole something. Did she pay for nail polish, Dad?"

He played with the rolled-up cuff of his white shirt for a second as he thought. Then he shook his head.

"No, she just bought some gum and a box of mashed potatoes," he said

"Are you sure there was no nail polish, Mr. Chan?" Remi asked.

He nodded, the light glinting off his shiny bald head.

I turned to Remi. "Goldilocks ate the porridge!"

He nodded. We bolted after the thief.

CHAPTER TWO

"Thief!" I yelled at the back of Samantha's head. "Stop!"

She hesitated then took off. Remi sprinted past me. He was like the rookie in a cop show trying to make a name for himself, and I was his doughnut-eating partner trying to catch my breath as I lumbered after the two.

Our suspect had a half-block head start and was almost as fast as Remi. I wondered if her guilt made her run faster as she rushed past the hotel, the sub sandwich store, the alleyway between the two buildings, the post office, and the tire store. A train rumbled across the railway crossing just past the flower shop and cut off her escape route. She hesitated for a second, then rounded the corner of the flower shop. Remi glanced back.

"Go down the alley!" he yelled. "Cut her off. I'll drive her your way."

I skidded to a stop, doubled back to the alley and scrambled along the gravel roadway. As I ran, I peeked between the houses for any sign of my partner or the suspect. About four houses down, I spotted a shadowy figure crouched between two houses. It had to be her. I climbed over a chain-link fence and landed in a backyard. Woof!

The shadowy figure turned out to be a black pit bull who did not like unannounced visitors. I backpedalled and slipped on something slick. The dog's owners didn't clean up after their dog very much; probably because they were scared to go near the sharp-toothed beast. I scrambled along the grass, avoiding the pit bull's minefield until my back hit the metal fence.

The dog lunged at me. I shut my eyes waiting for the bite, but it never came. When I opened my eyes, I noticed a heavy, silver chain leading from the barking dog's collar to a rusty piece of rebar jammed into the ground. The pit bull couldn't get at me. He strained at his leash, trying to pull himself an inch closer, but the chain held tight. I could almost smell his foul breath as I scrambled to my feet and hopped the fence back into the alley. The dog continued barking at me, while I dusted myself off.

The sound of footsteps caught my attention. Samantha was running toward me.

"Stop right there," I yelled, triggering more barking from the dog.

She skidded to a halt. Then she spun around and ran away. I chased her. She was too fast for me and she knew it. She even shot me a parting sneer as she reached the end of the alley. Suddenly, from out of nowhere, Remi tackled her and brought her down on the thin strip of lawn by the sidewalk. She flailed and kicked, but my partner held on.

"Let me go," she screamed. "Help! Help!"

"Shoplifter!" Remi grunted. "We know you stole the nail polish."

"I did not," she yelled.

They continued shouting at each other, attracting the neighbours who began to gather in the alley. One old lady came out in a fuzzy pink bathrobe with bunny slippers. An old man with a farmer's hat rolled himself forward on a silver walker. I informed the two that we had nabbed a shoplifter, and then I joined my partner as he pulled Samantha to her feet.

"Turn out your pockets," I ordered.

"No," she growled.

"We know you stole the bottle," Remi said.

More spectators came into the alley, like bystanders gathering at the scene of a car accident. Samantha noticed them and clammed up. Remi got a good grip of both her arms.

"It's okay, everyone. Nothing to see here. Move along," I explained, acting like a cop clearing a crime scene.

The bystanders murmured and stepped back, but they didn't leave. The old man with the walker complained, "Today's kids have no respect."

Samantha turned bright pink.

"Search her pockets, Remi."

He reached down, but hesitated when he noticed her tight black jeans. He pulled his hand back and glanced at me, his face turning as pink as Samantha's.

"Put my hands in there . . . how . . . maybe you should do it." Remi steered her toward me.

My face grew warm as I looked at the skinny pants, wondering how to get my hand inside without touching our suspect's thigh.

"Empty your pockets," I said. "Or else we'll get the police to do it."

She pouted, looking to the crowd for support, but they were as curious as I was to see what was in her pockets. We were an audience waiting for the magician to produce a rabbit out of her hat, or in this case, a bottle of nail polish from her pocket. Judging by Samantha's frosty glare, she wanted to make us disappear.

"Fine," she said. "Let go of me."

Remi reluctantly loosened his grip. She reached into her front pockets and turned them inside out. Empty. The magic act was going down the tubes, but I wasn't going to leave until Samantha produced something.

"Back pockets," I barked.

She turned around, lifted the back of her T-shirt and showed me the butt of her dark jeans. No back pockets. Maybe she was a real magician. Remi nudged my ribs.

"I bet she threw the bottle between the houses," he suggested.

I turned to the crowd. "Can you help us find a bottle of pink nail polish? It might be in your backyards."

The crowd split off to search for the stolen bottle, while Remi and I stood guard over our suspect in case she pulled a disappearing act. Samantha said nothing. If this were one of our favourite cop shows, she was exercising her right to remain silent.

"We're going to find the bottle," I said. "You might as well confess now. We'll go easier on you if you do."

Remi shook his head. "No way. We're going to throw the book at her. Call her parents. Call the cops. Maybe even call the *Bouvier Herald*. I bet we could get a front-page story out of this."

Like the many police shows we watched, my friend was playing bad cop to my good cop.

"Take it easy, Remi," I said. "This is her first offense."

"Doesn't matter. Your dad should make an example out of her." He then launched into a talk about how shoplifting was going to lead to worse crimes and her life would be ruined. "It's a bottle of nail polish today, but next thing you know, you're stealing an iPod or a set of speakers. Then you're breaking into old ladies' homes so you can kidnap their cats and hold them for ransom."

Samantha folded her arms over her chest and rolled her eyes.

I backed up my partner. "Doesn't matter, Remi. She won't get that far. When my dad presses charges, she'll have a permanent police record. That means everyone will know she's a criminal. She'll never be able to live it down."

She looked down at the ground, refusing to make eye contact. We had her. It was just a matter of time before she talked.

"Confess now and we'll go easy on you," I said.

"Don't talk and we'll throw the book at you," Remi threatened.

"That's enough!" boomed my dad. He stood behind us, his hands on his hips and the wisps of his remaining hair blowing in the breeze. "You two are supposed to be working."

"But she stole some nail polish," I said.

Remi nodded. "Are you going to press charges, Mr. Chan?"

"You have no proof," Samantha said, daring us with her narrow eyes.

"Did anyone find the bottle?" I yelled.

No one answered. Not a single spectator returned.

"Let her go," Dad said.

"But she's guilty," I pleaded.

Samantha shrugged. "All I wanted was to get some mashed-potato mix for my mom."

"I know she stole something," I said. "I can prove she's a thief."

"Me? I'm innocent." She flashed a sweet smile that made me want to vomit.

Dad turned to me. "Back to the store," he said, his voice low and menacing. I knew he meant business.

"Yes, Dad," I said and started to turn toward the store.

Just as I turned, I spotted Samantha's smug grin, but I said nothing. Remi shuffled behind us. When we were out of earshot, he leaned forward. "Marty, are you sure she took the nail polish?"

"I know when someone's guilty," I whispered.

"Tell your friend to go home," Dad barked. "We not need him."

"How about tomorrow?" I asked.

"Not any more. He's fired."

Remi started to say something, but Dad grabbed my arm and pulled me away like he was hauling a crying toddler away from a toy box. As I was being dragged away from my best friend, all I could think was that this was all Samantha's fault.

CHAPTER THREE

All night, I tossed and turned thinking about how Samantha pulled off the theft, and I realized that the only person who could tell me was her. The trick was to get her to talk and I had a plan. In the morning, Remi was waiting for me by the school equipment shed, our detective office. He shot rocks at the wooden door with his hockey stick.

"Sorry about my dad," I said. "He kind of overreacted yesterday."

He took another shot. "No kidding. I was used to your mom yelling at me, but not him."

"I think we can get you back in the store."

He rested his hands on top of the hockey stick. "How?"

"We need Samantha's confession."

Remi sighed, and lined up another rock for a shot. "We'd have a better chance of getting you on the Oilers' starting line."

"That's why we need an undercover agent."

He lined up another shot. The rock pinged off the centre of the shed door, leaving a nick in the wood.

"Remember how the Mounties went undercover to catch the accomplice to that bank robbery in Edmonton last year? They posed as criminals and infiltrated the bike gang. Then they got one of the real bikers to spill the beans. We need someone to trick Samantha into confessing."

Remi scooped a rock up on the end of his stick and balanced it in the air. "Good idea. Who do you have in mind?"

"Follow me."

I headed toward the schoolyard. Grade three students were crawling over the bright green playground equipment like flies on mouldy bread. Near the school building, a grade five boy dangled a dead mouse in front of a group of grade five girls. He chased the girls around while he swung the mouse by the tail like a hypnotist's watch. Their shrieks and his laughter filled the air until he lost the grip on the mouse's tail and it smacked him in the face. Then, he started to shriek as shrilly as the girls he had chased.

He ran into the school trying to brush the mouse germs off his cheeks.

Meanwhile, the grade six students leaned against the school's brick wall and acted too cool for kiddie games. A few of the girls texted on their cell phones — probably to each other since cell phones were not allowed in class. A couple of guys were playing Nintendo DS — another device not allowed in class. Our principal only wanted us to use the ancient machines in the library and the computer, most likely because he could monitor what we were doing on them, while he couldn't see what kids did on their cell phones.

A few guys snickered at mouse boy as he squealed past them. The dead mouse was most likely one of the family of mice that had taken over the school and fell victim to the custodian's rat poison. Scrawny Ben Winston eyed another corpse on the cement pad, then glanced at the group of texting grade six girls and inched closer to the furry corpse.

Away from the girls, Trina Brewster leaned against the wall, reading a thick book. It was probably something about vampires, her favourite subject. Her long blonde hair was pulled back with a black clip. She stood a head taller than most of the boys, which was not the case last year. Her growth spurt over the summer had made her a prime candidate to become a basketball star if it weren't for the fact that she hated basketball. She liked the contact sport of hockey. I had the bruises from our street hockey games to prove it. She could take care of herself in any situation, and that made her the perfect undercover agent.

As soon as she spotted us, her freckled face lit up. She broke away from the wall. The breeze swirled around her yellow dress, which fluttered up enough to show off the dirty jeans she wore underneath. I was pretty sure that by the end of the day, the dress would be just as messy as her pants. As I watched her walk toward me, the moisture left my mouth and found a new escape route in my armpits. I like-*liked* her and I knew she had like-*liked* me, but for the sake of our friendship with Remi, who also like-*liked* her, we agreed to just be friends. If only my heart went along with my head. I gulped, trying to force my feelings from hiccupping to the surface.

"Trina, you're never going to guess what happened," I said.

"I caught a shoplifter," Remi blurted.

"*We* caught a shoplifter," I corrected.

"But I did the hard part. She was a runner."

"I was the one who cut her off," I argued. "And I almost got eaten by a rabid pit bull during the chase."

"Really? You didn't tell me that."

"All true."

"Well, I was the one who tackled her and I have the scratches to prove it."

"You were too chicken to search her pockets," I said.

"I didn't see you rushing to put your hand in her pants."

"I would have."

"Would not."

"Hel-*lo*," Trina cut us off. "I'd like to hear the story sometime this week. Does one of you bubbleheads want to tell me, or do I have to read it in the *Bouvier Herald*?"

I recounted the crime. Remi interjected with comments about how he tackled Samantha. I knew he was trying to impress Trina. I explained that we didn't have evidence, and my dad fired Remi for fooling around on the job. She patted Remi's arm in sympathy. A pang of jealousy jabbed beneath my ribs.

"We're pretty sure Samantha did it," I said. "We just have to get her to confess. That's where you come in, Trina."

She bit her lower lip and looked away.

"What's wrong?" Remi asked. "You'll do it, won't you?"

"Samantha and I used to be friends," she said. "Are you sure she stole the nail polish? Maybe she moved the bottle to a different shelf."

I shook my head. "She took off when we chased after her. If she didn't take anything, why would she run?"

"I feel like I'd be betraying a friend."

Remi moved closer. "You two haven't talked in over a year."

"I didn't say she was my best friend, but I still don't like to rat out anyone."

He whispered. "I hate rats too, but she stole from Marty's store."

I nodded. "No friend of yours would ever do that, Trina. You can't let her get away with stealing from my dad."

Trina thought for a minute, then said, "She can't know I had anything to do with it. You promise?"

I nodded. "That's why it's called undercover work."

She scrunched her dress in her right hand as she looked at the two of us. Finally, she nodded. "I'll do it."

"Okay, let's get started," Remi said, clapping his hands together.

"Hel-*lo*, I can't go up to her and say, 'I know we haven't said two words to each other in a year, but let's be BFF' I have to give her a reason to trust me."

"Trina's right," I said. "Start slow and work your way into her trust. That's the way the cops do it on TV."

Remi grumbled, "Fine, fine, but let's get started now."

"Where is she?" Trina asked.

We scanned the wall where only scrawny Ben lingered near the dead mouse. Everyone else was gathered at the far end. There was no more interest in cell phones or Nintendo games.

"I think I see her," Remi said. "Other side of the crowd."

Trina walked toward the commotion. The last of the kids left the wall and joined the mob. Curiosity was like the flu — able to spread quickly. Remi and I caught the fever and headed over to see what the fuss was about. In the middle of the crowd, Nathan Black instructed Eric Johnson and Kennedy Anderson to hold a wooden board between them. The two boys pushed their bellies into the board and gripped the plank with their hands, while the curly haired Nathan made a slow-motion chop action at the board like he was practicing his aim. The kids were mesmerized as Nathan repeated the motion as if he were underwater.

He was a new kid at school, but he didn't suffer from any of the shyness that came with most new kids. He was always calling people by their last name as if he didn't have time to learn their first names. His family moved to Bouvier at the start of school. He announced in the first day of class that he was a karate expert. Eric Johnson didn't believe him, so the next day Nathan brought his black belt to class. To me, it looked like a bathrobe belt, but Nathan claimed the dark cloth made him a karate expert. The following week, he brought a trophy to school and claimed the silver-plated karate figurine on the top of the trophy should have been gold, because he won first place. There was no name on the trophy. I didn't know if he was telling the truth. He assumed that I was also a master of the martial arts. When I told him I wasn't, he refused to believe me, claiming martial arts were something in my genes.

The stocky dark-haired boy surveyed his audience, then he raised his hand, showing off a white bandage wrapped around his palm. The crowd let out a collective "ooo."

"A word of warning to you all. I can do this because I trained at my father's dojo. It takes normal people years of training to do this, but my dad said I'm special."

The kids oohed and aahed. At the other end of the group, Trina edged beside our suspect. She tugged on her earlobe, signalling she was about to make contact. I tugged on my earlobe and scratched my armpit, which meant go ahead.

"Ahem . . . it seems the master has something to say," Nathan said, who had spotted me in mid-scratch. "Do you have thoughts on how you would break the board?"

Everyone gawked at me. Nathan narrowed his gaze. Behind him, beanpole Eric struggled to hold the board while pudgy Kennedy wheezed from the effort of holding his end.

"I didn't say anything," I said, shrinking behind Remi.

Trina piped up, "He was making fun of you. I overheard him earlier."

I gaped at her, my jaw dropping. Beside her, Samantha smirked. The kids let out a collective "ooo". Nathan's nostrils flared wide open.

Remi rushed to my defence. "Marty was talking about my last hockey game."

Trina grimaced and then launched into another attack. "I heard Marty say that black belts are only good for holding your pants up."

The kids gasped. Nathan clenched his fists and took a step forward. Trina whispered in Samantha's ear and got a harsh laugh in response. She was using me as a way to get closer to our suspect. I hadn't expected her tactics would involve getting me beaten to a pulp.

"Do you have any more words of wisdom for me, Chan?" he asked, gritting his teeth.

"Ah . . . ah . . . a true warrior fights himself when he loses control of his feelings," I said.

I recalled a similar lesson being taught in a kung-fu movie I saw a few months ago. I hoped Nathan had seen the same movie. His eyes went wide with anger, but he stopped.

"And when you fight yourself, you always lose," Remi added, driving home the point.

Nathan said, "If the master is done with his games, I'd like to continue."

I kept quiet.

He returned to the board. He pressed his hands together in a praying position and closed his eyes. "One . . . two . . . three . . . the flower petals are opening in spring. Four . . . five . . . six . . . the caterpillar turns into a butterfly . . . seven . . . eight . . . kittens in a sunbeam . . . "

Trina interrupted, "Nathan, let Marty break the board if he thinks he's so good."

Beside her, Samantha snickered and nudged Trina with her shoulder. Trina was making headway, and I had to help her get in tight with our suspect.

"Why don't you break the board, Trina?" I said. "All you'd have to do is step on it with your big clown feet."

Samantha looked down at Trina's shoes. The kids snickered.

Kennedy whined, "Will someone show us how to break this board so I don't have to hold it any longer?" Behind his thick glasses, his green eyes were giant marbles. His spiky brown hair reminded me of a pudgy version of Sonic the Hedgehog.

"I'm not breaking anything," I said. "It's just a stupid board."

Nathan opened his eyes. "Chan, please respect those of us who embrace your culture."

"Karate is Japanese," Remi said, "and Marty is Chinese."

"Same difference."

Eric, still holding the board, shouted, "Yeah, they all look alike."

"No, they don't," Remi said, standing up for me.

No one heard him over the kids' laughter. I hated being the butt of jokes, because it reminded me of how hard it was to fit in. I fired back, "Nathan, everyone knows the only reason why you have a black belt is because your father owns the dojo."

The kids let out an eager gasp. He ground his foot into the pavement, grinding a few pebbles under his sneakers. "No one insults my father's dojo. Apologize now."

A hush fell over everyone. Their waiting stares reminded me of basketball fans watching a free throw. The ball bounced off the rim and hit the backboard then circled the rim. Everyone waited for the ball to fall through the hoop and they waited for Nathan's reaction. He headed toward me. I backpedalled until my back slammed against the wall. I pushed my back against the bricks, hoping the nuns who once used the school as their convent had built a secret entrance in the wall, but all I felt was the hard surface and some wads of gum. I was pretty sure I was going to become one of those crushed wads.

CHAPTER FOUR

According to my grade six teacher, Ms. Nolan, a Spanish matador tested his courage by facing down a bull in an arena. With only a bright red cape, the matador stood cape-to-horns against the snorting creature. The giant beast tried to rip the cape and the matador to shreds. Nathan was the bull and I was the matador.

"Do you know what I can do to you?" he asked. I was pretty sure that no matter what I answered, he was going to show me.

He leaned so close I could smell what he had for breakfast — toast with peanut butter and milk. I scrunched my face from the stench. "Apologize."

I said nothing.

"No apology, no mercy," Nathan said as he stepped back and took a karate stance. His hands looked like bull's horns. The cheering kids made me think of a bloodthirsty crowd in the stands of a bullfight. The only thing missing was the red cape. Suddenly, I realized I wasn't the matador. I was the cape that the bull was about to gore. Nathan wiped his thumb across his nose and tugged one leg of his cotton pants to expose his deadly sneaker. He ground his foot on the cement pad as if he were crushing a bug. Then he inched closer.

"Gentlemen, do we have a problem here?" a man's voice called out. It was Principal Henday, the man we all called The Rake, but only behind his back.

Nathan straightened up and stepped back. "No. We were just acting out a scene from a Bruce Lee movie. Isn't that right, Chan?"

As much as I didn't like Nathan, I was more afraid of The Rake. Our reedy principal made up for his slight stature with a heavy attitude about fighting. He was always ready to make an example out of any kid who tried to throw a punch.

"Yeah, we were just playing around," I said.

Principal Henday fixed me with an even look as he dragged his skeletal hand through his hair. I remembered he had brown hair last year, but the stress of the job must have turned his hair grey. The grey made him look more menacing, like a vampire. A starving vampire who needed to feed, and I was the main course. "Tell the truth, gentlemen."

Nathan closed his eyes and meditated. I could almost hear him counting: "one, two, three, kittens in a sunbeam." The Rake folded his arms over his grey suit jacket and began to tap one finger against his elbow as he drilled his stare into my brain. This was his finger of doom, a very effective way to get kids to talk. All he had to do was tap his finger and wait for a confession. The longer the tapping, the harder it was to keep quiet. One time, Eric Johnson caved to the interrogation and confessed to wetting his bed. Such was the power of the finger of doom. I tried not to look at the finger and kept my mouth shut.

Finally, The Rake stopped tapping and said, "No fighting of any kind in this school, real or pretend. I catch you doing this again, and it will be a strike against you both."

The Rake loved baseball, because he was forever handing out strikes to "bad" kids. Three strikes and the kid was out. In this case, we were given a walk. Nathan glared at me and headed off. The Rake went into the school. Remi came up behind me and patted me on the back.

"Oh man, I would have caved. The Rake freaks me out. How'd you stay so cool?"

"Mind over matter," I said, using my sleeve to sponge off the sweaty lake from my forehead.

Nathan joined his two helpers. Kennedy tossed his end of the board to one side. It landed on Eric's foot.

"Ow. Watch it, knob head," Eric barked.

Kennedy whined, "It was too heavy."

Nathan grabbed the board. "You'll have to build up your stamina if you want to work out in my dad's dojo."

"I'll try harder," Kennedy said. His chubby cheeks were red from the exertion of holding up the board. "Maybe I can do some odd jobs around the dojo and just watch you work out. Or what if I help you count? One . . . two . . . three . . . I'm peanut butter on a jelly sandwich . . . "

As the trio walked away, a part of me wished that I had fought Nathan. I replayed the scene in my mind: Nathan the snake master against the Marty the eagle lord. He twitched his body, giving away his first move, a punch, which I easily dodged. He was off balance. I ducked low and knocked him off his feet with a leg sweep. He fell on his butt and I launched myself into the air like an eagle and tumbled three times, before landing with my feet on either side of his fallen body, my fist screaming to his face like angry talons. I stopped an inch away from his face.

He screeched like a little girl and begged for mercy, while everyone cheered. I let him up and warned him to never challenge me again. He slithered off into the tall grass.

Remi interrupted my kung-fu daydream. "Mission accomplished." He pointed across the schoolyard, where Samantha and Trina were chattering as they walked toward the school entrance.

"Good," I said.

"Watch your back," Remi warned. "I don't think it's over."

"He wouldn't do anything else," I said. "Not with The Rake around."

My friend shook his head. "The Rake can't be everywhere."

I nodded and glanced at Nathan, making a note to keep an eye on the "karate master" in case he tried to teach me another lesson. Remi and I headed into the school. I hoped Trina was making progress with our suspect.

In class, I tried to eavesdrop on Samantha and Trina as they talked in hushed tones at the back of the room. I craned my head back so that I could hear. Mikayla Jackson, the grade six grump, must have thought I was spying on her.

"Back off, lurker," she barked.

She slammed her grey journal shut and glared; her short brown hair bristled as a warning. She scowled, flashing a mouth full of metal that looked like they could tear through pop cans. The other kids called her Jaws, but no one dared say that to her face because she had a fiery temper.

"I wasn't looking at . . . I mean . . . it's just that," I tried to explain.

"I don't care about your reasons. Click on another website. This one is 403 — forbidden access."

Suddenly, the entire classroom went dead silent. I glanced past Mikayla at our grade six teacher, Ms. Nolan, staring at us. With her long red hair and bright smile, I thought she should have been a model or a movie star instead of a teacher. I think she thought the same thing, because she was always cranky. She lived up to her name, Nolan, because her classroom was a place we called "No Land", which was inhabited only by her "NOs".

"No, don't stop on account of me. By all means, keep talking and cutting into my lesson time." She had a sarcastic sense of humour. She claimed her jokes were going to prepare us for junior high school.

Mikayla slowly turned around in her desk. "Sorry, Ms. Nolan."

"With your permission, I'd like to continue teaching. That okay with you?"

Mikayla hunched over and stretched out the back of her red T-shirt, which read: Byte Me. I was pretty sure she wanted me to get a good look at the slogan.

"Marty?" Ms. Nolan asked.

I knew better than to answer her rhetorical question. If you answered a rhetorical question, you'd turn red in the face like I did once when I answered Ms. Nolan's rhetorical question, "Do you take me for an idiot?" The answer to the question was definitely not "yes".

Eric hadn't figured out our teacher's sense of humour yet: "Keep talking, Ms. Nolan. That way we don't have to learn about computers."

The kids laughed. Our teacher aimed her sharp sense of humour at Eric like a pirate turning her sword on an enemy. "Did you say something, Eric? Oh? You're volunteering to be my dance partner when we do the dance unit," she said, making Eric walk the proverbial plank.

"I didn't say that," he protested, shaking his head so hard his blonde hair whipped back and forth like ragged sails against gale force winds.

Ms. Nolan stabbed hard and swift. "That's so sweet of you. Your mother says you have twinkle toes, Eric."

The roar of laughter that filled the classroom sounded like a crew of mutineers on a ship. Ms. Nolan tried to coax the burly Eric out of his desk to dance with her.

Eric waved her off. "I'm sorry, Ms. Nolan. I take it back. I didn't mean anything. Please don't make me dance with you."

"I think we can start class now . . . unless I have more dance volunteers." She looked right at me. I ducked down in my desk. I figured I had made enough enemies for one morning.

CHAPTER FIVE

L unchtime couldn't come fast enough. I hoped to catch Trina at recess for an update, but she and Samantha disappeared in the girls' bathroom for most of the break. Remi was busy showing a few of the French kids how to get good snap on a wrist shot, so I had no one to talk to except Kennedy, who decided to latch on to me.

"Who do you think would win in a fight? Jet Li or Jackie Chan?" he asked, wheezing as he tried to keep up with me. His breath smelled of chocolate.

"I don't know, Kennedy. Why don't you ask Nathan?"

"I did. He said Jet Li, but I didn't believe him, because I heard Jet Li became a Buddhist, and those guys don't fight. What do you think?"

"Why do you think I'd know?"

"Because you're Jackie Chan's nephew," Kennedy said.

"We're not related."

He glanced around the hallway and whispered. "It's okay. I know you have to keep it secret, but I won't tell anyone. You can tell me the truth. I mean he must have taught you some sweet moves, right? Right?"

"We just have the same last name," I said.

"Sure, sure, I get it." He winked at me. "You're not related at all. If I keep your secret, will you show me some of his moves? I just want to be able to defend myself. I promise never to use any of the moves except in extreme emergencies or when the teacher's not looking."

Kennedy pestered me for the rest of recess and for most of the morning, until Ms. Nolan finally moved him to the head of the class. As soon as the lunch bell rang, I slipped into the hallway and ducked out the door without grabbing my lunch bag. Missing out on lunch was a small price to pay to get him off my back. I rushed into the schoolyard and headed to the school shed, where I hoped to meet up with Trina and Remi.

Remi showed up a few minutes later, but there was no sign of Trina. I scoped out the schoolyard for her, but I could only make out Kennedy pestering Nathan about karate lessons. I pulled back from the bushes, while Remi was tearing his ham and cheese sandwich in half. He handed me one of the ragged halves.

"Thanks, Remi. I'll split my lunch with you at afternoon recess."

He cocked his head to one side. "Did your mom slip more octopus tentacles in your sandwich?" He was still leery of my sandwiches after my mom decided to make me a seafood salad using leftovers of shark fin, octopus and jellyfish. Remi set a world record for fastest spit take.

"No, I made it myself," I said. "No seafood. You know what I'm looking forward to next year when we get into junior high school? Cafeteria food."

"Monique said it's not all that great," Remi said.

"Your sister's a vegetarian. Of course she wouldn't like it, but me, I'd be ordering hamburgers and fries every day. What about you?"

"Two burgers. Extra fries."

"Yeah. But you know the coolest thing about junior high? We get to take classes together."

He mumbled. "Depends on a couple of things."

My friend's odd reaction worried me. He eked past grade five with help from Trina and me, but we hadn't been studying as hard this year. I wondered if he wasn't going to pass grade six.

"You want to get together after school today and go over math homework?" I asked.

His face twisted like I had just shoved a lemon into his mouth.

"I don't mind, Remi."

"Shhh," he said, putting a finger to his lips. "I think I hear something."

He peeked around the corner of the shed. He straightened up and motioned me to step back. Before I could move, Trina and Samantha came around the corner.

"Marty, your turn to hide," Remi said, tugging at his ear to signal me to go along.

"Sure thing. You found me pretty easy this time. Oh, hi Trina."

Remi asked, "You girls want to play hide and seek?"

"Yes, Trina," I said. "I hear you're pretty good at going *undercover*."

"Maybe Samantha should hide first," Remi suggested.

Trina shook her head. "She knows what you're doing. I told her everything."

Remi gaped at our undercover agent. I scratched my head. Had she gone so far undercover that she was now working with Samantha? Our cover was blown.

"Whatever Trina said to you is a lie," I said.

Samantha looked at me. "She said you were the best detectives she ever worked with."

Remi and I shared a look of wide-eyed surprise. I turned to Trina, silently asking for some kind of explanation.

She offered one: "I thought it was better for you to hear straight from her. Samantha, why don't you show them?"

Our suspect slowly nodded. She stepped forward and reached into her pocket. She withdrew the stolen bottle of pink nail polish.

"I'm sorry I took this," she mumbled.

Remi jumped up and down. "I knew it. I knew she stole it. You ditched it in one of the yards, didn't you?"

She shook her head.

"Then where did you hide it?" I asked.

Samantha slipped the bottle under her wide wristband until the entire bottle disappeared from sight. Remi let out a low whistle and nodded in admiration as he examined the wristband.

"Clever," I said. "Good job, Trina. We'll take it from here."

She shook her head. "Hear her out, Marty."

Samantha pulled out the bottle and handed it to me. Most of her black makeup had been wiped away and her moist eyes glistened in the afternoon sunlight. "I would have paid for it, but I didn't want anyone to know."

"Know what?" Remi asked.

Silence.

"She wanted to change her look," Trina answered.

"Why?" he asked. "I thought it looked cool."

Samantha mumbled, "You're the only one. I've been teased for the last month."

I shook my head. "Principal Henday has a no-bully zone. No one would dare do anything at school."

Trina put a finger to her lips. I said nothing more.

"It's not at school," Samantha said. "It's at home."

Remi let out a snort of disbelief. I let out a harsh laugh, but cut it short when I noticed Trina giving me a dirty look.

"Samantha, do you expect us to believe that you're being bullied at home for the way you look?" Remi asked.

I added, "Your mom telling you to dress nice doesn't count as bullying."

"It's not my mom."

"Who is it, then?" I asked. "Your dog?"

Remi chuckled. Trina shushed me.

"It's a cyber bully," she answered.

No one said a thing. Cyber bully was an easy term to remember. I knew the bully part all too well. The cyber part was what gave the bullying a cruel twist. Cyber bullies could pick on their victims through the internet. At least with a real bully, you were safe at home. With cyber bullies, home was the worst place to be, unless you didn't have a computer, because they could send you messages anywhere and at any time. Often, they hid their identities. Some kids believed this was because schools had strict no cyber-bully policies, but I believed it was because cyber bullies were cowards.

"Why don't you go to Principal Henday?" I asked. "He'll track down the jerk."

Samantha shook her head. "I can't. It's complicated. If he saw what the cyber bully was making fun of, well . . . I . . . I . . . "

Trina patted her on the shoulder, "Maybe it's easier if you show the guys."

She nodded and reached into her pocket to pull out her cell phone. She turned it on as Trina beckoned us to gather around the tiny screen.

"The cyber bully zeroed in on a video that Samantha posted on YouTube," she explained.

Remi crossed his arms. "Wait a minute. That could be anyone. It doesn't mean someone at school is the cyber bully."

"That's what I thought at first, but you'll see why it has to be someone from school in a minute."

He leaned in closer, blocking my view. I shuffled to the other side of Samantha and got a clear view just as she loaded the video on her cell phone. On the tiny screen, Samantha was dressed from head to toe in a black hoodie and jeans. Judging by the rumpled blue blanket on the bed behind her and the closet full of black T-shirts and jeans behind it, I guessed she was filming the video in her bedroom. The lighting was dim, but I could make out her face, which was pale except for the black eyeliner and black lipstick. Electronic music started over the video and she began to sway to the music, losing herself in the moment. Then she flipped off her hoodie and zoomed into the camera as she started to sing. She didn't sound bad, but it was hard to make out the lyrics because the music was too loud. I thought I heard her sing, "Don't let him put you down; he's nothing but a clown."

She danced away from the camera, and bent low while she sang something that sounded like, "Thinks he's in charge of you, but there's nothing he can do." I wondered if she was singing about her dad after he gave her curfew or something, but it all became clear when Samantha stood up, holding a garden rake. Taped to the green tines was a picture. It was hard to make out the face, but the rake gave away the identity. She was singing about Principal Henday.

"The video was up for about two days when the cyber bully started posting. He made fun of my outfit, mostly, but sometimes, he'd write things about how I sang like a strangled cat. I posted a comment to tell him to shut up or I'd tell, and he wrote that I'd never talk or else he'd share the video with Principal Henday. Every day, he'd send some snarky comment about my hair, my makeup, my fingernails. I couldn't take it any more and I removed the video, but he kept hounding me about how I looked, and I thought the best thing to do was just change my look. That's why I took the nail polish. I thought it would stop him."

Nothing stopped a bully. The Boissonault twins taught me that much. When they were at school, they picked on me every day. Sometimes, they made fun of my eyes and how they were slanted. Other times, they said my hair looked too weird. Once, they teased me for the black armband I had to wear after my grandmother's funeral. Even if I could change the way I looked, the brothers would find another reason to pick on me. Bullies don't need a reason. They need victims.

"I'm sorry to hear about the cyber bully, Samantha," I said.

"I want you to make him stop. I want you to work for me."

"You want to hire us?" I asked.

Trina smiled and nodded.

"How much?" Remi said.

Samantha stiffened. "Trina, you said they'd do it for the experience."

"I'll talk to them," Trina said.

But as our partner turned to us, I heard a rustling noise coming from the bushes behind Samantha. Someone was watching us.

CHAPTER SIX

I was the only one who noticed the movement. Trina was too busy consoling Samantha, and Remi was shaking his head at me.

"No way we're going to help a thief," he said.

"If you want me to pay, I will," Samantha pleaded.

"I got fired because of you," Remi accused.

"Please help me. You're my last hope."

I tried to signal Remi to look to the bushes, but he was more interested in making Samantha feel bad. The spy could hear everything we said, and I was pretty sure this had to be the cyber bully. I inched toward the bushes as if I were sneaking up on a feral cat, pretending not to notice anything was there.

"No money," Remi said. "I want my job back."

"She can't get you that," Trina said.

"Maybe we should talk this over, Remi," I said. "Over here."

"Hang on a sec."

"I'm sure she can do something else, right Samantha?" Trina said.

"No, it's this or nothing. Get my old job back, and we'll take your case," Remi said.

Samantha rubbed her arm, nervously. "Are you sure that's the only way?"

"Yes. Right, Marty?"

I turned from the bushes, trying to be as casual as I could so I didn't tip off the spy. As I sauntered toward the gang, I tried to wink at Remi.

"Something in your eye?" Samantha asked.

"Yeah, I think some dirt blew in it," I said as I twitched my head toward the bushes.

Remi caught my move. He winked back at me.

"Now what's wrong with Remi's eye?" she asked.

"Um . . . dirt blew in it," he said.

"But there's no wind."

"That's because the shed is blocking it from you," I explained, winking at Trina.

"Are you two trying to pick me up?" Samantha asked.

Trina jumped in, picking up on the signal. "Forget them. I'll solve this case myself. We don't need them. Marty, Remi, you two can go."

"Fine, we will." I said. "Let's go, Remi."

We turned around and headed toward the bushes. I angled to the left, while Remi moved to the right. There was no movement from the foliage. Had the spy caught wind of us? No time to waste: "Move, move, move!"

He ran to the bushes, while I headed toward the other escape route. Trina charged after us, leaving a puzzled Samantha by the shed. Remi and I rounded the bushes, but there was no one there.

"Did you get him?" Trina asked.

"Nope. He's gone," I yelled.

"What's going on?" Samantha demanded.

I explained, "I thought I saw a spy behind the bushes."

"Are you sure you saw something, Marty?" she asked.

Trina raised her eyebrow at me. "Well, are you?"

Remi answered for me. "Found some footprints here. They look fresh."

"Check the schoolyard!" I ordered my partners. "The spy couldn't be that far away."

Trina didn't have to be told twice. She sprinted to the schoolyard, while Remi and I followed. Samantha took up the rearguard and poked me in the back.

"Do you think it was the cyber bully?" she asked.

I nodded as I scanned the field. Mikayla sneered at a group of grade four kids playing tag. Nathan was showing a karate move to a confused Kennedy, who panted from the exertion of holding up one leg in a kick stance. Eric Johnson jogged away from the shed toward a couple of grade six girls who were seated on the field texting each other. Ida Eisengram, the grade five teacher's daughter and my arch nemesis, brushed something from her jean-jacket sleeve. The spy could have been any one of them. I motioned my partners to head back to the shed.

Samantha scratched under her wristband as she watched us come back. "Well, do you know who was spying on us?"

I shook my head. "But we have a list of suspects."

"Looks like you just hired yourself some detectives," Remi said.

Trina patted my shoulder. "We have a case."

"Remi, check out the treads of the footprints," I suggested. "It's a good lead."

"On it."

"What should I do?" Samantha asked.

"Confess to my dad and get Remi his job back."

She chewed her lower lip and glowered at me from behind her lopsided bangs.

"That's the price. Take it or leave it."

After school, Samantha came to the store to confess. She stood between Mom and Dad with her head hung low. It was like the final scene of a cop show where the criminal was finally caught but in this real-life scene, I was going to see the sentencing and the punishment. Samantha fidgeted from foot to foot as she waited for Dad to say something. Her confession had been met with stony silence. Dad eyed the ancient bottle of nail polish. He rolled his eyes at Mom, who was scooping out the remains of ice cream with a dill pickle. She could have rested the tub of ice cream on the beach ball that was now her pregnant belly.

"We should call the police," Dad said as he rubbed his balding head.

Samantha's eyes bulged. Her mouth opened, but no words came out. She was a first-time thief about to get a harsh sentence normally meant for hardened criminals, and I was her reluctant defence attorney coming to the rescue.

"She came in and confessed," I argued. "You gave the last two shoplifters a break."

"We need to teach the kids a lesson," he said.

"I'm sure she's sorry. Isn't that right, Samantha?"

She finally found her voice. "Yea . . . yea . . . yeah. M . . . m . . . my mom was furious with me. She was too embarrassed to come, but she told me I had to return the bottle and apologize for what I did. I promise I'll never steal from your store again. I'm so, so, so, so, so, so, very sorry."

Mom shook her head, the pickle now dangling from her lips like a mouldy cigar. Her curly, black hair looked like a nest of snakes hissing at Samantha. "Sorry, not good enough. Too many of you bad kids stealing all the time."

"Mom, she's a friend," I jumped in.

The Medusa hair seemed to hiss at me. "What kind of friend?"

"Um . . . ah . . . a friend at school," I said.

"A girlfriend?" Mom chomped the pickle in half.

Samantha and I both shouted "No way."

Samantha added, "He likes Trina."

"Not any more."

Dad folded his arms and let out a snort of disgust. "Marty, your friends should know better than to steal from you."

Samantha said, "I'm really, really, really, very, very, sorry."

"Don't talk to my son," Mom said. "She no good for you, Marty."

"We're just friends," I said.

"Too young for girls," Mom muttered.

"Mr. Chan, Mrs. Chan, I'll make it up to you. Don't call the police. Please."

Dad stroked the stubble on his chin as he eyed Samantha, who was on the verge of tears. "You work in store for a month to make up for what you did."

"Yes sir," Samantha said, wiping her eyes.

"And you pay for the nail polish," he added.

"I will."

Mom's eyes narrowed as she scrutinized Samantha.

"Does that mean Remi can get his job back?" I asked.

Dad shook his head.

"Why not?"

"She work for free," he replied. "Now get her to mop the floor."

"Come on, I'll show you where the bucket is," I said. He would give Remi his old job back but only if I convinced my friend to take a drastic cut in pay.

I leaned close and whispered, "You got off easy."

Too close for my mom's liking. "She not here to play."

"I'll work hard, Mrs. Chan."

Mom finished the rest of the pickle and said nothing. She looked at Dad, who shrugged. "Marty, you show your friend where the mop is."

I smiled. "This way, Samantha." I said.

We headed to the back of the store. As we walked, I thought I heard snakes hissing. Mom was following us, sucking air through her pursed lips. She locked in on the back of Samantha's head like a missile ready to launch on its target. I picked up the pace. In the storage area, I hauled out the mop bucket and showed Samantha how to fill it with water.

"You guys better solve the case fast," she whispered.

"No talking," barked Mom.

I filled the bucket. The sooner I set Samantha up at the store, the sooner I could join Trina and Remi. They were supposed to check Samantha's YouTube video and email at the Bouvier Public Library while I finished my chores. Now that I had to train Samantha under Mom's supervision I'd never get out. Mom coiled around us like a boa constrictor. I glanced at Samantha, who looked like a scared rabbit caught in the crushing grip. Sometimes it was better to be a mongoose than a rabbit.

I leaned closer to Samantha. "Your hair smells nice," I said.

Mom barked, "Too close."

"I'm showing her how to mop the floor," I said. I picked up the mop and invited Samantha between my arms so that I could show her how to swish the mop head. She wouldn't step into my arms, so I had to move toward her.

"What are you doing?" she asked as I put my arms around her.

"Trust me," I whispered, then I said loud enough for Mom to hear. "Put your hands on the mop handle and let me guide you."

"Enough!" With cobra speed, she moved in and snatched the mop away from Samantha and me. "I teach her. You go."

"But there's so much she has to learn," I protested.

"I do it."

"Fine," I said, feigning disappointment. "Can I go to the library to study?"

"Yes, you go away. Don't come back until this *gwai mui* is gone," Mom said.

She called Samantha the white girl, but the way she said it sounded more like an insult than a fact. I knew she was going to sink her fangs into Samantha and extract any information about how she felt about me. I was glad to get out of the viper's nest. Samantha looked at me with big eyes, silently pleading for help. I felt sorry for her, but not enough to stick around.

Trina and Remi were huddled around one of three computer stations in the Bouvier Library. A teenaged boy sat at the other computer, playing an online zombie game. He wore headphones that were plugged into the computer tower and he seemed to really be into shooting the undead shambling around the monitor.

On the other side, an old woman squinted at the monitor of the third computer. The town library's computers were more fun than the school's computers. Here, kids could sign up for time to play popular online games or surf the internet. That was probably the reason there were two teenagers waiting their turn for the computers. The teens flashed me dirty looks as I joined my partners.

On the screen was a website advertisement for spy equipment.

"What's this about?" I asked. "You're supposed to be working on the case."

Remi motioned me to keep quiet as he glanced at the hawk-nosed librarian glaring in our direction. She lifted a finger and pointed at the "Silence is Golden" sign next to her counter.

"The librarian's cranky today," he explained as he nodded to the teen with headphones. "He had the volume on full blast and didn't know it."

I whispered, "What are you looking at?"

Trina smiled. "We thought we should get real equipment for our detective work."

She pointed at a page of wireless lapel microphones that could be hidden under a shirt. There was a pen camera that could sit in a pocket and capture everything through a tiny lens on the cap. I even saw a bug that looked like a bug with an ad that read, "Be a fly on the wall". Remi scrolled down the screen and stopped at a remote-controlled surveillance tank with a video camera mounted on the turret.

"Oh, man, this is what we need," he said. "We can pretty well spy on anyone with this baby."

"Hel-*lo*, did you see the price?" Trina asked.

Remi wouldn't give up. "We could pool our savings. And when I get my job back at the store, I'll be able to cough up some extra money."

"Yeah, about that, Remi . . . "

My friend turned back to the screen and pointed at the spy tank. "Don't you think this would be the coolest gadget?"

While the tank would be good for detective work only, it could also be used to track the prairie dogs by Remi's trailer home.

"How much do you have now?" I asked Remi.

"I can cover about half," he said. "How about you?"

"I have ten bucks," I said.

"Ten bucks?!"

Trina clamped her hand over Remi's mouth and glanced at the counter, where the librarian and the waiting teens glared at us.

Remi asked, "Why so little? After all the work you do in the store."

"My parents don't pay me. Dad says that I work so I can have food on the table and a roof over my head."

Trina chuckled. "My dad's always telling me the same thing."

"Come on, guys," Remi said. "Do you want to be serious detectives or not? Oh, cool, it comes in blue too."

"I think Remi might be right. The website says the mike can pick up a whisper. It has everything we need," I argued.

Trina shook her head. "We can't afford the tank. Ooo, how about this?"

She clicked on the image of a teddy bear Stuffy Spy. Remi and I groaned. The teenagers coughed in our direction.

One complained, "They're not even using the computer. When is their time up?"

Trina shot back, "We booked it for twenty minutes. We still have five minutes left."

The librarian cleared her throat. "Not if you continue talking. In fact, it doesn't even look like you're using the computer."

"We're using it," I said. "I have to check my email."

I pushed my friend out of the seat, sat at the computer, and called up my email program. At least we looked like we were doing something at the computer. I cracked a smile at the cranky teens as I typed in my password and waited for the program to load.

"We can afford the Stuffy Spy," Trina said.

"I can also afford to buy broccoli, but you don't see me buying it," Remi said. "Marty, ask your parents for the money to get the tank."

"Actually, I think you might have to take a pay cut at the store . . . "

"What?!"

The librarian swooped down on us. "Your time is up."

"We still have two minutes," Trina argued.

"Hurry up!" one of the teens yelled.

"Back of the line for yelling in the library," the librarian shouted. Apparently, she was allowed to yell, but we weren't. "As for you three, your time is up. Now."

"I have to shut down my email," I said.

When I looked at the monitor, my mouth dropped open. The inbox was full. Most days, I was lucky to get one email and usually it was from some banker from a far-away country offering me a hundred-million dollars, if only I would give him all my personal information. These emails were definitely not from that friendly and desperate banker. The subject heading of the first message read:

"Slanty-eyed, ching-chong is nothing more than a dilly ding-dong."

This nasty note was the first of many.

CHAPTER SEVEN

The email lingered like the bitter aftertaste of cough syrup. I tried to fill my mind with happier images like playing road hockey with Remi or the smell of Trina's hair, but nothing washed away the hateful words I had just read. They made me feel confused, angry, ashamed and guilty. Most of all, I felt helpless against the cyber bully, because he hid behind a fake email address, which gave me no chance to answer his cruel words.

I wanted to see the rest of the messages, but at the same time I didn't want to look. It was like picking at scabs that I knew would only get worse if I touched them. Still, I couldn't resist. I moused the cursor over the next header.

"You don't have to read the messages, Marty," Trina said.

"Yeah, this guy's a monkey butt," Remi added.

"Why would they write this about me?" I asked. "I never did anything to anyone, did I?"

"You did nothing wrong," Trina declared. "Think of the emails as clues that point to the cyber bully."

Remi said, "I don't think he wants us to find him. A real bully wants to take on the wimps. That's how he can prove he's tough. This guy doesn't want to come out in the open, because he knows he doesn't have the muscle to back up the mouth."

I shook my head, "He knows Principal Henday will kick him out of school if he gets caught. This guy's smart."

"A bully is not smart," Trina argued. "They're dumb. Always."

I wrote my name on the computer sign up sheet and took my place in line. At the computers, three teens wearing headphones played video games. They looked like they were going to use every second of their time.

"We'll find him, Marty," Remi said.

"We don't even know what he looks like. All we have to go on is what he wrote."

"Let's look at the messages," Trina suggested.

Remi rubbed his chin. "I bet this guy's a scrawny peewee. A real bully would write something like, 'On Tuesday, I'm going to pound you into hamburger', or 'On Thursday, you're going to be deader than chopped wood'."

I looked at him as if he had just sprouted a second head.

"Say what?!" Trina exclaimed.

From the back of the library, the librarian shushed us. Her beady eyes peered at us from over a stack of books on her counter. I pointed at Trina and the librarian shook her head. When she turned away, Trina smacked me on the arm. I let out a silent scream.

Remi whispered, "Marty, don't tell me that she hurt you with the punch."

"Hel-*lo*, you'd be crying if I hit you," Trina said.

He shook his head. "Doubt it, monkey butt."

"Hel-*lo*, you'd be calling for your mommy."

"Wait a minute," I interrupted. "Say that again."

"Monkey butt?" he whispered.

Trina scowled. "Hel-*lo*, he was talking about what I said."

"No," I said. "I mean, yes."

"Monkey butt?" he asked.

"Hel-*lo*, he doesn't need to hear that again."

"Yes, I do."

Trina raised a questioning eyebrow at me, while Remi scratched his head.

"Remi, you always call people 'monkey butt', and Trina, when someone says something you think is dumb, you start your sentences with 'hel-*lo*.' Don't you guys get it?"

They shook their heads.

"Maybe the cyber bully has a word or a phrase he uses, like monkey butt or hel-*lo*. If we look through the messages, we might find a clue to the cyber bully."

"Not a bad idea," Remi said.

"You're smarter than you look," Trina joked.

We waited for the teens to finish their games. I checked the clock and inched closer. The teens smelled funky, like B.O., even though they were all just sitting at the computers. I winced and moved away, hoping the librarian would kick them off for stinking up the place.

"What's your password?" she asked.

"G . . . R . . . the number eight . . . B . . . O . . . I."

"Great boy? I thought it'd be Momma Bear," Remi quipped.

I wasn't in the mood to laugh. Trina logged into my inbox. The headers filled the entire computer screen. The cyber bully had sent fifty-five nasty messages. Trina clicked on the second email, which read:

"You smell like rotten bananas."

I stepped back from my partners and secretly took a whiff of my armpits. No funky smell. I shook my head. I couldn't believe that one nasty note could make me doubt myself. The terrible thing about the emails was that the messages were permanent. If a bully told me the same thing at school, I'd only have to hear it once, maybe twice. The stain of his hurtful words might stick to me like dry-erase marker, but I'd be able to clear it away eventually. The hateful words in my email were as fresh as the first time I read the message. Sure, I could delete the message, but there were another fifty-four messages ready to take its place.

"Open the next one," I said, gnashing my teeth.

Remi tapped me on the shoulder and said, "Let me and Trina do this."

She agreed. "The messages might get worse."

"I'm okay," I said. "Check the email address. Maybe that'll give us a clue."

Remi sat down beside Trina and scanned the monitor. All the emails were coming from a user named 'ayedanosbst'. Trina grabbed a scrap of paper beside the computer and jotted the name.

"Keep going through the messages, Remi," she said. Then she got up and stretched. "I need some space to think. Come with me, Marty."

I shook my head. "I want to see the rest of them."

"I wasn't asking." She grabbed my arm and pulled me to a corner of the library, where the librarian was pushing a cart of books to a bookcase. She raised an eyebrow at the two of us, then pulled a pencil out the bun of hair at the back of her head and scribbled something on a card.

"Maybe there's a clue in the name," Trina suggested, holding up her slip of paper.

"It looks like gibberish."

"It might be an abbreviation."

"I don't think so," I said. "Most computer abbreviations are short. Like 'RT' for retweet or 'LOL' for laugh out loud. This is too long to be an abbreviation."

"Well, it has to mean something. Do you want to help me decipher this name?"

The one thing I was good at was breaking up words to find their meanings. Usually, the words were real and not a random collection of letters. Trina put her thumb over the word, hiding parts of the letters. The only words she could make were "aye" and "dan".

"Does that mean anything to you?" she asked.

"We're looking for a guy named Dan who might be a sailor," I offered.

"Maybe it's like a personalized license plate where you can make a message with the letters."

"Or, maybe the guy's cat walked over the keyboard when he made up his user name."

Trina rolled her eyes and placed the scrap paper on one of the book shelves. She covered up the first half of the word. 'Bst' meant nothing to me, but Trina wrote down the letters, leaving a space between the 'b' and the 'st'.

"What if we put a letter between those?" Trina wrote the letter 'e' so that the word became 'best'.

I shrugged. "Dan is the best at being a sailor?"

The hawk-eyed librarian peered between the books on the shelf and whispered, "The library is no place for passing love notes."

I blushed. "We're not. I mean, we were . . . but not any more."

Trina's face also turned a bright pink. We were saved when Remi called out, "Done."

Trina slipped away, abandoning the note. I followed, glad to get away from the librarian's watchful eyes.

"What did you find?" Trina asked.

"The cyber bully used one strange word all the time."

"What?" I asked.

"Well, it makes no sense, but he 'maxi-means' a lot of things. Every third email, the cyber bully writes 'I maxi-mean it.'"

"That's a good start," Trina said.

I agreed. "We should check if Samantha's messages have the same word."

Trina logged on to Samantha's email. She clicked on the inbox folder and all Samantha's messages scrolled up on the screen. There were 1,476.

"This is going to take a while," Trina said, as she clicked on the first email.

"Is there any way we can just look for the emails from the cyber bully?" Remi asked.

She nodded. "We just have to search for emails from the address. What was it again?"

"Hold on. I'll get it." I headed back to the bookshelf and reached for the paper, but the pencil had rolled over it and covered part of the word. Everything became crystal clear when I read the part of the name that was uncovered — "Ayeda".

I knew the identity of the cyber bully. I headed back to my friends with the paper.

"Guys, I know who the cyber bully is. Look at the first part of the name."

Remi scratched his head. "Yeah? So?"

"Say it aloud," I said.

Trina did. "I . . . da. Ida." Her eyes popped wide open with recognition as she read the rest of the name aloud. "Ida . . . no . . . nose . . . best. Ida knows best. It's Ida Eisengram."

Chapter Eight

I da was the thief our detective team had caught last year. She was the daughter of my old grade five teacher, Mr. Eisengram, and a whiz at all things scientific, but she was also the grumpiest, meanest, toughest kid in all of grade six. Even Eric and Nathan knew to stay out of her way. She definitely fit the profile of a bully. Trina had a theory that Samantha might have snitched on Ida during her tattletale phase at the start of the year. She had ratted out Nathan Black for bringing nunchuks to school, Eric Johnson for cheating, and Mikayla Jackson for hacking into the school computers.

The next morning, Trina looked for Samantha to find out what she did to anger Ida, while Remi and I headed to our prime suspect. Ida sat by herself at the far end of the schoolyard. She had positioned herself far away from her dad, who was on supervision. Mr.

Eisengram was the centre of attention of the grade five students who adored him because he let them call him Mr. E. His bright white hair, neatly-pressed brown suit, and neon-green tie lit up the schoolyard like the moon on a dark night. His daughter was the exact opposite with her dyed black hair, scruffy jeans, ratty black hoodie and get-off-my-planet attitude.

Beside me, Remi was beaming ear to ear. Of all our detective work, interrogation was his favourite, especially the good-cop, bad-cop routine. We were going to be the bad cops. Trina was going to play good cop and coax a confession out of Ida. She lurked by the fence, waiting for the chance to swoop in.

As we drew nearer, I whispered to Remi, "Would you like to do the honours, sir?"

He grinned as if he had just found out his parents won the lottery. "Why, thank you, sir. I would love to, sir."

Before he could take another step, Ida spotted us and bolted. I sprang into action and sprinted after her. She pulled further ahead of me as I huffed and puffed along the fence. If we were vehicles, she was a Ferrari and I was a little red wagon with only three wheels. There was no way I was going to catch her. On the other hand, Remi was a Porsche. He blew past me. Ida continued along the fence, dodging past bushes and little kids. At one point, I thought she was going to get help from her dad, but as soon as she saw him, she veered to the left and headed around the other side of the school. She slowed when she spotted Nathan showing Kennedy and Eric his black belt. Remi snagged the back of her hoodie and hauled her back.

"Where do you think you're going?" he asked.

"Let go before you rip the material," she demanded.

Nathan and his bunch looked our way, but I waved them off. "It's . . . it's . . . okay," I wheezed. "Nothing to see here."

Remi grabbed Ida's arm. "Why did you run from us?"

"I didn't like the smell of you," she said.

"Do I smell like rotten bananas?" I asked.

Ida scrunched her face up. "No. You smell more like a lapdog. Both of you."

"What are you talking about?" Remi said.

"Don't play stupid. I saw you guys talking to Samantha yesterday."

"So you were spying on us," I accused.

"Oh come on, it was plain as the big nose on Remi's face that she's trying to get you guys to do her dirty work for her."

Remi went on the offensive. "We know you're cyber bullying her."

"What? You're serious? Is that what she told you? She's lying."

"Yeah, right," I said. "We know about the messages. Why are you picking on Samantha? Did she snitch you out? Did she look at you the wrong way? I figure someone like you doesn't need much of a reason, eh?"

"You want the truth? If the devil coached basketball, Samantha would be his star player. She's the one who's been bullying me."

"I also saw the emails you sent me, Ida," I accused. "You gonna say that she sent those too."

Her mouth dropped open. "What emails?"

"You get straight A's in every subject, so you don't get to play stupid now."

She shook her head. "I have no idea what you're talking about. What emails?"

Remi stepped in. "Things will go easier if you talk to us now than if you talk to The Rake. We know you sent all those emails."

"I don't know what emails Marty got, but if you want to see the messages Samantha sent me, you're more than welcome to read them. I have them all right here." Ida reached behind herself and pulled her cell phone from her back pocket. She turned it on and called up her emails. There were nasty notes telling Ida she was a teacher's pet and a snob. Some told her to go play in traffic or take a short jump off a tall cliff. None of the messages were kind. The sender name was "SamanthaSays."

Was this a case of tit-for-tat? Had we landed in the middle of a schoolyard feud? I didn't know what was going on, but I knew we had to get to the bottom of it all. "We need to talk to Samantha."

Ida nodded. "I'd love to say a few things to her."

We marched across the field to the school, where Trina was waiting for us. She informed us that Samantha didn't remember snitching on Ida, while I filled her in about the new messages. Trina cast a cautious look in Ida's direction.

"Are you sure they're from Samantha? Maybe Ida is faking it." Trina spoke loud enough for Ida to hear.

"That's what we're going to find out," Remi said.

We confronted Samantha by her locker about the emails and she denied everything. The two girls glared at each other like two boxers facing off against each other in a boxing ring. Remi stepped in between them before they could go at each other.

"She's the cyber bully," Samantha accused. "Tell the principal about her."

Ida shot back. "And he'll suspend you as soon as he sees your emails."

"I didn't send you any messages," Samantha protested.

"Your user name is SamanthaSays, isn't it?" Remi asked.

"Yes, but those aren't my emails," Samantha said through gritted teeth. "Ida's the cyber bully."

"She's lying," Ida accused. "I have the proof in my inbox."

"So do I."

"You're the one who's bullying me."

"Pick on a teacher's daughter? Do you think I'm an idiot?"

"Samantha's got a point," Trina pointed out. "If you're going to pick on someone like that, you'd probably want to do it in a way that she'd never find out. Why would she use her own email account?"

"Wait a minute," Ida said. "You think she's smart enough to do that, but I'm not?"

Remi stepped between the pair. "No one's saying that."

"I don't even know Ida's email address," Samantha said.

"I don't know your address either," Ida shot back.

He waved the girls back. "One of you did it."

"Unless what we have is false evidence," Trina suggested.

"What's that?" my friend asked.

The first time I heard the phrase was on a cop show. The police had found proof that was fake and nearly arrested the wrong woman for a crime. I always thought the phrase was weird because evidence was supposed to be a fact. How could something real be false? The two words were opposites.

Ms. Nolan said writers sometimes butted two opposite words together to create an oxymoron, which was basically nonsense that made sense. I remembered the definition by the last half of the word, "moron". Two words with opposite meanings pushed together would sound moronic or silly. How could Kennedy Anderson be a butt head when his two body parts were at opposite ends? How could a Ninja turtle be fast if it was a turtle? How could wrestlers step into a circle when it had four corners? In this case, how could the emails be false evidence?

"Was there any weird word Samantha used in emails, Ida?" I asked.

"No. I don't know."

"Did you see the word 'maxi-mean'?" Remi prompted.

Ida shifted her eyes back as she mentally reviewed the messages. Then she looked at us. "Yes, now that I think of it. There were a couple of times I saw that."

"Interesting," Trina said.

"What's so interesting?" Ida asked.

I explained. "Two different people wouldn't use the same odd word in their emails. The cyber bully who wrote the messages is the same person. And if the emails are coming from both your accounts, then it must mean the cyber bully knows how to log on to your account."

"Impossible," Samantha said. "I haven't given out my password to anyone . . . except you guys."

Ida shook her head. "The only person who knows my password is Ms. Nolan, and she keeps it on her computer with all the other passwords."

A piece of the puzzle fell into place for me. "Okay, if the passwords are on the computer, maybe the bully hacked in. Know anyone who did that lately?"

All at once, everyone exclaimed, "Mikayla."

We would have set the world's record for jinx punches, but I didn't think this was the right time to start smacking people in the arm. Samantha and Ida wanted to confront Mikayla right away, but Remi held them back.

"We don't know for sure she's the one. This is a theory," I said, "and we have to get proof before we confront anyone."

Samantha calmed down, but Ida ranted, "I'm going to tell her that her eyes are too close together and her breath reeks of rotten cabbage. I'm going to tell her she dresses like a disaster victim. I'm going to tell her that the reason she has no friends is because she picks her nose and eats her snot and no one wants to be near the slime zone."

"You can't go to her yet," Trina said.

"Trina's right," I said. "If Mikayla is the cyber bully and she knows you're onto her, she'll erase the evidence. You won't be able to prove a thing and she'll get away with it. We want to stop her. Let *us* deal with the cyber bully."

Remi nodded. "Let the professionals handle this."

Trina touched Ida's shoulder. "I don't know what she wrote about you, but I'm going to make sure the cyber bully gets what she deserves, but only if we get the right person."

Samantha backed her up. "If it weren't for them, we'd still be hating each other, Ida. Let's give them time to get to the bottom of this."

She reluctantly agreed. "Fine, but I get first crack at her when you solve the case."

"Okay," I said. "Now let us do our job."

The pair walked down the hall, leaving our team to sort out the next steps of the case.

"So, how are we going to do this?" Remi asked.

Trina and I looked at each other. I was hoping she knew, and I think she was hoping I had the solution. We said nothing for a few minutes.

Finally, he piped up. "Well, why don't we spy on her when she's on the computer?"

"Hel-*lo*, I think she'll notice us peeking over her shoulder," Trina said.

"She's right," I added. "We'll have to be invisible."

"I wish we could be like a fly on the wall," he said.

"Or a Stuffy on a desk," I said.

Trina smiled. Remi nodded. "Good idea, Marty."

CHAPTER NINE

We ordered the Stuffy Spy over the internet, which meant we were at the mercy of the delivery service. While we waited for the Stuffy Spy to arrive, Trina and I traded clichés about waiting. A watched pot never boils. A watched computer program never loads. A watched kid never eats his vegetables. The days turned into a week and the weeks turned into a month. The spy equipment was supposed to go to Remi's house, because he convinced his mom to use her credit card to order the gear.

Every day at school, I asked Remi if the Stuffy Spy had arrived and his answer was always no. I saw him less and less, because he had hockey practice and Samantha had replaced him in the store. Trina got busy with soccer practice. The only person who had time for me was the cyber bully. Every day, she sent a new round of messages. I was glad I didn't have a computer at home, but I dreaded having to log on to the computer at school.

The only thing worse than the emails was Mom, who decided that I had to work for her because Samantha was doing my job. I offered to help Samantha, but Mom refused, claiming the girl needed to be punished. My new job was to rub Mom's feet while she sat on the couch and watched Chinese soap operas on TV. As I listened to melodramatic Chinese actors and tried not to breathe in Mom's funk-alicious toe jam, I wondered if Samantha wasn't the one who got off lucky.

Finally, the fateful call came. I was in the middle of digging gunk from between Mom's toes with a cotton swab when Remi phoned. Mom reluctantly took her feet off my lap so I could answer the phone in the kitchen.

"The furry eye has blinked," Remi whispered.

This was the secret signal that the Stuffy Spy was in. We had to speak in code on the phone because Mom liked to eavesdrop on my calls. I was pretty sure I could hear her breathing on the other line.

"Oh no. Are you sure? The school project will be ruined, and Ms. Nolan said the project was due tomorrow," I said loudly enough for Mom to hear.

"You'd better get here quick," Remi said. "Or else you're going to fail."

I spoke into the phone. "Mom, can I go?"

From the other room, she yelled, "Yes. Next time, start earlier."

I hung up and returned to the couch, where Mom was fishing the last dill pickle out of a giant glass jar. I was sure the baby was going to come out greener than my lime-green corduroy pants.

"I wish I could stay, but I have to get a good mark."

Bits of pickle flew across her belly as she answered. "You come back fast. You cut my toenails next."

I shuddered as I looked at her dirty toenails. Off I went.

At Remi's place, Trina and I gathered around the stuffed teddy bear. The brown and white bear looked like any other stuffed animal. It wore a cute pink-and-blue ribbon tie and its forepaws were stretched out to hug someone. The only weird thing was one of its shiny black eyes seemed to follow me wherever I walked in the room.

Remi tapped the eye. "That's the camera lens. The mike is here." He tapped the Stuffy's snout.

Trina leaned forward and spoke into the bear's nose. "How sensitive is the mike?"

"Awesome. I had the Stuffy Spy in the living room and it picked up my sister making out in her boyfriend's car," he answered. "You can save the recordings in its butt."

He pulled open the teddy bear's rear end and revealed a black flash drive. He pulled out the tiny stick, which was only slightly larger than a stick of gum.

"How much memory does it store?" I asked.

Trina picked up the instruction booklet and skimmed it. "Enough for two hours of video and audio. Not bad."

"And the recording can be set to be motion activated," Remi added.

"Wicked," I said.

"The really cool thing is this." Remi plugged the flash drive back into place and picked up a remote control that looked like a portable video game player. The tiny monitor was dark.

"Why did it come with a remote control?"

"Watch."

Remi set the Stuffy on the floor and motioned us to follow him into the living room. We gathered around the remote. The monitor flickered to life. On screen was Remi's messy bedroom floor.

"Amazing," Trina said.

"It gets better," Remi said, smiling. He pushed the joystick and the image moved around the room.

Remi zoomed in on his jockstrap and then zoomed out again.

"You can control the camera?" I said. "That is awesome."

Trina asked, "What's the range? Can we control it from outside the school?"

Remi shook his head. "Maybe the next room or from the hallway, but no further."

"That's okay," I said. "We'll set up a communications relay. Remi you can work the camera. Trina and I will use the walkie-talkies to make sure no one sees what you're up to."

Remi beamed. "I can't wait until tomorrow to try this out for real."

"Why do you get to work it?" Trina asked.

"You guys don't know how," he said. "I have more experience."

"Hel-*lo*, you just got it today."

Remi said. "I ordered it. I use it."

"You'll break it before we get it to school," Trina said. "Remember what you did with your Nintendo DS?"

"That was a toy. This is a spy tool."

"Hel-*lo*, you said you used it to spy on your sister. If she catches you, we won't have a Stuffy Spy tomorrow. We'll just have loose stuffing."

"She won't catch me."

"Hold on," I said. "There's only one way to solve this. Rock, Paper, Scissors."

Remi perked up. "Always with the good ideas."

Trina grunted. "Whatever."

"You guys ready?" I asked.

My friends nodded and we started to play Rock, Paper, Scissors to decide who got to play with the remote control. Rock smashed scissors. Scissors cut paper. Paper covered rock. When only two people played, it was easy to figure out a winner, but with three people going at the same time, there were many arguments about whether rock smashed scissors before paper covered rock. This resulted in do-over after do-over. One-hundred-and-seventeen rounds later, Remi's parents kicked us out so they could have dinner, making Remi the winner by default.

The next day, Samantha and Ida took up a position at the one of the two school entrances, so they could watch out for any kids coming into the building. If someone came in, Samantha was supposed to create a distraction while Ida warned Remi. Trina took up a guard position at the other school entrance, which was also where I'd be stationed.

First I had to plant the Stuffy Spy near Mikayla. She was working at a computer in the school library. I sat down next to her and slipped my navy-blue backpack off my shoulder. When she saw me, she bared her braces in a grimace and used her body to block the monitor. I picked up a book and pretended to read. She started to type, ignoring me. I yawned, unzipped my backpack and reached inside for the Stuffy Spy.

Mikayla peeked at me. I stuffed the bear back into the backpack and flashed a sheepish grin. She narrowed her eyes and slowly spun back to the computer screen. I pulled out the bear and placed it on the table, trying to position it so the camera could pick up what was on the monitor.

She turned again. I hugged the bear and flashed a cute smile.

She furrowed her eyebrows. "Can I help you?"

"Nope. Just doing some reading."

"Oooo . . . .kaaay." She returned to her work on the computer.

I angled the Stuffy Spy on the table and slowly backed away. It looked perfect. I crept out of the library. In the hallway, I gave Remi the thumbs up. He took a seat beside the door and pulled out the remote control as if he were playing a video game. I taped the talk button down on the walkie-talkie so I could hear Remi's report and handed him the device. Mikayla stared at me through the door's window, but I pretended not to notice as I scampered down the hall.

Trina gazed out the window of her guard post as she tapped the wall nervously. Outside, the boys were playing chicken wars in the schoolyard and the girls were laughing at the fallen chickens. No one was interested in coming inside. Almost no one. Kennedy lumbered toward the school entrance.

I bolted away as he opened the door. "Stall him."

He tried to move past Trina, but she blocked his way. "Sorry, but you're going to have to use the other entrance."

"But I have to go the bathroom right now," he said.

"The custodian said she just mopped the floor and she doesn't want anyone making tracks."

"The other entrance is all the way around the other side. I don't know if I'll be able to make it." His voice faded as I got further away.

Around the corner, I lifted the walkie-talkie and turned it on, hoping to warn Remi, but I realized his talk button was still taped down and there was no way I could contact him.

" . . . I think I see Mikayla's arm . . . I'm going to move the camera down. I think I see her butt. Ew, there's toilet paper sticking out her pants. I'm trying to get a fix on the screen . . . "

Suddenly, a new voice blasted through the walkie-talkie.

"Hey, Boudreau, whatcha doing?" The fact that the boy used Remi's last name told me who the speaker was — Nathan Black. Somehow he had slipped past Ida and Samantha.

"Um . . . playing a video game," Remi replied.

"Doesn't look like a Nintendo DS," Nathan said.

"It's not. It's Marty's. His dad got it from Hong Kong. It's a prototype. Very high tech."

"Mind if I look at it, Boudreau?"

"Buzz off."

Nathan said, "You might want to be a little friendlier. After all, we're going to have to stick together next year."

I had no idea what Nathan was talking about.

He continued, "We'll be the only Bouvier guys at the sports school. We hang out together, no one's gonna pick on us. We might be able to show the other kids who's in charge while we're at it."

"I've got enough friends."

"You mean Chan and Brewster? They're not athletes. Why would you hang out with them?"

"I like them," Remi said.

"I'm surprised they haven't dumped you now that they know you're going to the sports school in Edmonton. I figured they'd be hiring another bodyguard," Nathan said.

"Don't you have some boards you have to break?" Remi shot back.

"Why so defensive? I'm just saying I'm surprised they're still hanging out with you."

"I didn't tell them I was moving, and I don't want them to know. Not yet."

I couldn't believe what I had just heard. My best friend was moving away and he didn't bother to tell me. After all we had been through, he couldn't trust me with the most important news of his entire life. All I could think was why.

CHAPTER TEN

Remi's revelation was like drinking expired milk. Both made me sick, and I didn't know when the real pain would hit. I paced the hallway back and forth, debating whether I should confront Remi or leave him alone. Eventually, my pacing turned into wandering. What did I do wrong that my best friend would want to abandon me and not even tell me about it? I found myself near the school entrance, but I had no idea how I got there. The sound of Trina arguing with Kennedy pulled me out of limbo.

"In the time you took to argue about going this way, you could have gone to the other entrance," she said.

He countered, "Yes, but now I have to go so bad that I won't be able to hold it if I go to the other entrance. The floor must be dry by now."

"No one goes down this way."

"You'd better be careful, Trina," the pudgy boy warned. "I'm on my way to becoming a green belt in karate. You'd better not mess with me."

"The custodian was the one who gave the orders. Do you want to get on her bad side, Kennedy?"

"Mrs. Podanski gave the orders? Um, no, that's okay. I'll go the other way, but if I don't make it, she's going to have to clean up another mess." He stormed out the door.

Trina looked back at me. "Something wrong with the mission?"

"No."

"Then why do you look like someone just took your slice of birthday cake?"

"Did Remi say anything to you about where he's going to school next year?"

She shrugged. "Same place we are, I assume. The Bouvier junior high. What's that have to do with the stakeout?"

"Nothing," I said. "Never mind."

Suddenly, my walkie-talkie squawked. Remi's voice barked at us. "Alpha One, come in. Alpha One, do you read me? Goldilocks is going to sleep in Baby Bear's bed."

"Remi's in trouble," Trina shouted. "Let's roll."

She tore off down the hallway. Did I want to help the friend who was going to abandon me without so much as a goodbye? I hesitated until Trina barked at me to move. I chased after her. When I reached the library, there was no sign of Nathan, but Trina was huddled near Remi staring intently at the monitor on the remote control.

"Well, one of us has to go in there," he said.

"She'll suspect something if we move the Stuffy Spy around," Trina pointed out.

Remi looked at me. "Mikayla's noticed the bear. She keeps looking at it. You have to move it into a better position."

"Why me?" I asked.

"You're the one who planted it," Trina said. "Make it look casual."

"There's nothing wrong with where the Stuffy Spy is," I snapped.

"Remi can't see the computer monitor."

"Not my problem."

"What's with him?" Remi asked Trina.

She shrugged. "Marty, if Mikayla looks too close, she'll spot the camera. It only makes sense that the guy who put the Stuffy down in the first place is the one who moves it. Mikayla will suspect for sure if anyone else does it."

"I'm not moving it," I said.

Remi checked the monitor again. "We have to do something soon. Look."

He held up the remote control. Mikayla's face filled the screen.

Trina grabbed me by the arm and shoved me into the library before I could utter a single word of protest. I skidded to a stop just inside the doorway. Mikayla sat back at her station and pretended she wasn't examining the teddy bear. I glared through the glass window at my partners, but they just shooed me forward. I shambled toward our suspect. She snuck a glimpse at me, then turned her attention back to the computer as I sat next to her.

"You have a cute teddy bear," she said.

"It's not mine."

"Oh?"

"It's a present."

"Lucky person," she said, staring at the monitor.

"Yeah," I said, nudging the Stuffy Spy closer to her.

She stiffened. "OMG, what do you think you're doing?"

My hand froze. I stammered, "M . . . m . . . making it walk. Growl. I'm Teddyzilla! Roar." I lifted the Stuffy Spy by the arms and made it walk like a toddler across the table.

Mikayla rolled her eyes. "Lame-oh."

"Roar! Me hungry. Me want to eat. Yum. Love to eat books."

She stared at me as if I had just picked my nose in front of her, but I couldn't stop. I had to get the Stuffy Spy into position and make sure she wasn't suspicious about it.

"Oh, now me tired. Want to sleep. Night-night." I lowered the teddy bear to the table and angled its head so that the camera eye was pointed right at the computer screen.

"You finished?" she asked.

I slapped my hand on my forehand. "Yikes, I just remembered what I came here for. Ms. Nolan needs a book. Can you watch the teddy bear? Why don't you put him in your lap while you're working? He won't mind." I grabbed the nearest book I could find and headed out of the library.

As soon as I reached the safety of the hallway, Trina gave me a high-five, while Remi adjusted the joystick to get a view of Mikayla. She squinted at us, her face filling the screen. Her eyes were popped wide open. I was sure she had spotted the camera. Her face disappeared. I glanced through the window and saw her put the Stuffy Spy down and move toward the door. Her steely grimace reminded me of the grill of a big rig, and she was on a high-speed collision course with us. No time to stick around.

"Run," I ordered.

"Why?" Remi asked.

"Goldilocks is on the warpath," I said.

Remi stuffed the remote control under his shirt and took off down the hall with Trina. I ran in the opposite direction, hoping to lead Mikayla away.

Behind me, she shouted, "Marty, come here. I want to talk to you!"

Her pounding sneakers on the tiled floor sounded like thunder. I hoped I would beat the storm. I picked up the pace and headed to the end of the hall. She continued to yell. I sprinted around a corner and screeched to a halt in front of the main office. I half-walked, half-skipped in front of the eagle-eyed secretary. There was a strict no-running-in-the-hall policy. She watched me over her black-rimmed glasses and tsked at me as she shook her head. Once I was past the office, I opened up and ran out the main doors.

Mikayla burst out of the school building after me. Wherever I ran, she was there. Behind the shed. Along the fence. Through the playground equipment. This girl was unstoppable. She reminded me of an old movie about a killer robot from the future called

The Terminator. I wondered if her braces were part of her robotic body, and I feared she might use them to shred me like grated parmesan cheese.

"Over here!" Remi yelled. He waved from the other school entrance. I headed toward safety, but Mikayla angled her approach and cut me off. She reached out for my arm. I pulled away, missing her by inches and sprinted into the school. Remi slammed the door shut and locked her out. I leaned against the wall and caught my breath, while she pounded on the window. She bared her metal braces and ordered us to open the door. She was definitely the Terminator; if not, at least a distant cousin. Finally, she stopped pounding and disappeared from the doors.

"Library! Quick!" I yelled. "Before she finds another way in."

We sprinted to the school library. Inside the room, Trina waited for us beside the computer. The computer was off and there was nothing around the station.

"Get anything, Trina?" Remi asked.

She shook her head. "She must have turned off the computer before she came after us. Wait a minute. Where's the Stuffy Spy?"

"I gave it to Mikayla," I said. "She set it down right here."

"Maybe she grabbed it after we ran," Remi suggested.

I shook my head. "She didn't have it when she was banging at the door."

Trina said, "Do you think someone else took it?"

"Don't the kindergarten kids come to the library around now?" Remi asked. "Maybe one of them grabbed it."

"Oh, great. We lost our spy gear and we still know nothing?" I asked.

"Not nothing," Remi answered. "When I was doing the stakeout, I noticed she plugged in a flash drive to the computer. Whatever she's doing must be on that stick. All we need to do is get our hands on that flash drive."

I grumbled, "Wouldn't need to if you worked the camera right."

"What?" Remi asked.

"Never mind," I said. "This stakeout's a bust." I stomped out of the library. I wanted him to follow me and tell me everything about this hockey school and why he kept it secret, but the only person who caught up to me was Trina. I glanced back. Remi walked the other way. I'd give him one more chance to come clean.

"What's wrong with you?" Trina asked.

"Nothing," I said.

I left her behind as I headed to the classroom. If I could throw myself into the investigation, I wouldn't have to think about what Remi did. As I entered the room, Mikayla was putting away her backpack. I watched for any sign of the flash drive, but she didn't pull it out. I decided to move in for a closer look, but I should have been watching my back. Nathan grabbed me in a headlock and dragged me into the room. "Who wants to see if Chan's ticklish?"

The boys in class rushed over and poked at me. I laughed as Kennedy found a ticklish spot in my ribs. Nathan cranked his headlock a little tighter. I grabbed his arm and tried to pull myself out, but he was too strong. He spun me around so I could see everyone in the classroom.

Mikayla cracked a huge smile. Nathan let go of me when Ms. Nolan entered the class. We scrambled to our seats. The entire afternoon, I could feel Mikayla's gaze on me. I was sure she suspected what we were doing. She was probably the spy in the bushes and the first chance she had, she'd erase her flash drive. The only way to stop her was to get my hands on the stick, but first I had to find out where she kept it.

At the end of class, she packed her gear into her backpack, leaving nothing in her desk. She was like a snail, carrying everything on her back. I started to follow her, but stepped on Kennedy's foot.

He yelped, "Watch where you're walking. You don't want to mess with a karate expert."

"Sorry, Kennedy."

He gave me a karate pose. "Hi-ya! I don't care if your uncle is Jackie Chan."

"Ease up, Anderson," Nathan said, clapping his hand on Kennedy's back. "You're not allowed to use karate in the school."

"Sorry, master." He bowed. The pair left the classroom together.

I followed them to the doorway and scanned the hallway for our suspect. Trina joined me.

"Any sign of the flash drive?" I asked.

She shook her head. "But I'm willing to bet it's in her pencil case."

The only thing Mikayla hadn't put in her backpack was a cherry-red pencil case. She clutched it to her chest as she headed to her locker.

"I wonder if Remi saw her put the stick in the pencil case. We should ask."

I shook my head. "He won't know." Truth was I didn't feel like talking to Remi. I wanted him to know what it felt like to be kept in the dark. Trina dragged me to the school shed. While she compared notes with Remi, I glared at my friend and waited for him to come clean about the hockey school. He didn't say a thing about moving to Edmonton. I'd give him one more chance. Just one more and that was it.

"How do we pry that thing from Mikayla's hands?" Remi said.

Trina suggested, "We could always steal the flash drive."

I shook my head. "Yeah right. She'll catch us before we get two feet with it."

"Not if she doesn't know it's gone," Trina said. "We just have to make a switch. Remi, what colour was it?"

"Black. It looked like the one in the Stuffy Spy."

"Great, so we just have to find the Stuffy Spy and pull out the memory stick," I said. "Oh wait, the Stuffy Spy is stolen."

"We can't swap out the memory stick, but we know she keeps it in her pencil case," Remi said.

"So."

"We could switch the pencil case."

"Not a bad idea, Remi," Trina said.

"Are you kidding me?" I asked. "She'll know we took it as soon as she opens the fake case."

Remi smiled. "We keep her distracted so she doesn't go into her case. Buy enough time to see what is on the memory stick."

Again Trina nodded. I hated that she agreed with him.

"And I suppose you just happen to have an identical pencil case?" I said, sneering at my friend.

He beamed. "No, but I'm sure we'll be able to find one at your dad's store."

Trina clapped Remi on the shoulder. I rolled my eyes. One more chance. I'd give him one more chance, but that was it. This time I meant it.

It took a couple of days to track down the right pencil case, but Remi found one in his sister's closet. He showed up at the secret shed with the decoy.

"It's not an exact match," I said.

"Close enough," Remi said.

Trina nodded. "We just need to buy some time."

He opened the case to show it full of pencils and erasers. Trina beamed, impressed. So did our new partners, Samantha and Ida. We needed their help to keep Mikayla distracted and they were more than willing to help bring the cyber bully to justice.

Trina outlined the plan. "You guys get the pencil case, pass it to me and then keep Mikayla distracted so I can check what's on the drive. Everyone got it?"

Ida asked. "Are you sure the proof is there?"

Trina nodded. "Positive."

The girls looked at each other and nodded to Trina. They headed toward the school. As they neared the kids, Ida grabbed Samantha's backpack.

"Keep away!" Ida yelled.

"Give it back."

Some of the girls sneered at the commotion, but the boys were like golden retrievers and the backpack was like a bright yellow tennis ball. Ida launched the backpack into the air and Nathan caught it. He passed the backpack to Eric Johnson, who hot-potatoed it to Kennedy. Within seconds, all the tongue-wagging grade six boys were playing keep-away from Samantha.

She played her part. "You are going to be sorry. Give that back. It's got important things in it. Don't drop it."

The boys laughed as they tossed the backpack to each other. Meanwhile, some of the girls inched closer. Mikayla ignored the action. I waved to Remi. He ambled behind the group of gawking girls and snatched Eloise Gervais' backpack from her shoulder.

"Keep away!" he yelled.

Eloise shouted, "Give it back."

Too late. Remi launched the backpack at the pack of grade six girls. It landed on the ground with a dull thud. Not one girl moved to grab it. If boys were dogs, girls were cats and it took more than a slobber covered tennis ball or Eloise's backpack to get them to move.

"Get Mikayla's backpack," I yelled. "I hear she's got licorice in it."

If they had tails, the boys would have been wagging them. They charged at Mikayla, who clutched her backpack and ran.

"I heard Helen's got a stash of chocolate bars," Remi added.

Some of the boys split off from the pack and chased Helen. Their yips and yaps were infectious and soon the girls were screaming louder than the boys. Every girl's backpack suddenly had something even more important than the last one. The girls scrambled around the schoolyard like ruffled chickens. The boys chased after them like dopy mutts. Outside the commotion was the fox, Trina. She waited for the right moment to strike. She tapped her watch and lifted her left hand straight up in the air. The signal.

I ran to Nathan as he tried to pry Mikayla's backpack from her hands. She had a Terminator grip on the strap. She snarled at Nathan and the other boys.

"Don't you dare."

She held her own against the guys.

"Tickle her," I yelled.

Kennedy picked up the challenge and poked at Mikayla's ribs. She squealed and instantly gave up the backpack to Nathan, who ran away with it. A half-dozen backpacks flew from boy to boy, while the kids scattered across the schoolyard.

Trina charged into the fray, heading straight for Nathan, who waved the backpack in the air. There were so many bodies and backpacks, it was almost impossible to tell who had what. Almost.

I yelled, "Toss me the backpack!"

He hurled it high over Mikayla. I caught the thing and ran away. When she came close, I tossed the pack to Remi. He hurtled between Ida and Samantha. Mikayla chased him, but the girls smashed together like prison gates and trapped her between them. Remi hurled the pack toward Kennedy, but made sure it sailed over the pudgy boy's outstretched hands and landed in Trina's waiting hands. The boys groaned and turned their attention to the other backpacks in play.

Now it was up to Remi and me to buy Trina the time to make the switch. As Mikayla disentangled herself from the pile up with Ida and Samantha, she searched the schoolyard for her pack. Remi and I jumped her and tickled her sides, sending her into a laughing fit. She howled at us to stop, but we kept poking her ribs and reaching for her armpits until she could barely breathe. We kept at it. I thought I saw tears rolling down Mikayla's cheeks as she howled. Everything was going according to plan.

Suddenly, there was a tap on my shoulder. I shrugged off the tap. Again, there was a tap; only harder. I turned. "What do you . . . " My words died in my throat.

Principal Henday towered over me. Mikayla's backpack dangled by the strap from his hand. Behind him, Trina shook her head at us. The mission had failed.

"My office," he bellowed. "Now!"

CHAPTER ELEVEN

Principal Henday's office felt hotter than a sauna, mainly because the thought of what he was going to do made me break out in a flop sweat. The back of my shirt stuck to the hard wooden back of my creaky chair. Beside me, Remi wiped his damp forehead with the sleeve of his Bobcat's hockey jersey. I wondered if his status as a star hockey player might save him.

The Rake leaned forward and rested his thin arms on the top of his rosewood desk. Then he began to flip through one of two file folders on the calendar blotter. He slammed his hand on top of the other folder. I jumped at the sound, which echoed off the dingy yellow walls of his cramped office.

"You gentlemen know what these are, don't you?" he asked, his deep voice filling the room.

I shook my head.

"They are your permanent files," he replied. "Any trouble you cause ends up in a file. Pretty frightening, isn't it?"

Sweat sealed my lips shut. He let the silence hang in the air, drumming his fingers on the file.

"This file will stay with you for the rest of your lives," The Rake said, shaking his grey-haired head. "This may be your last year here," he added, "but that doesn't mean your past can't follow you to your next school."

He let the threat hang in the air. I had hoped to start junior high with a clean slate. Judging by the way my friend stared at his shoes I think he was hoping for the same thing.

Remi asked, "What happens to the file?"

"I pass it on to the principal at your new school so he can separate the angels from the devils."

"Are you going to add what happened this morning to the file?" I asked.

The Rake leaned back in his chair and cracked a thin-lipped smile. "Mr. Chan, it's interesting you ask that question. Only a guilty person would ask a question like that."

I stared at my file.

"Did you start the shenanigans?" he asked.

I said nothing.

"Well, Mr. Chan?"

He began to tap his finger on the file. I learned to resist the power of the finger of interrogation, which worked well when kids were in grade four or five, but I was a grade sixer now and I was immune to the finger. The Rake must have sensed it, because he grabbed a pen and began to click it open and closed. Not quite tapping, but still effective. I clamped my lips shut, hoping he wouldn't write anything

"The only thing worse than causing trouble is failing to take responsibility for it."

Remi mumbled, "What kind of trouble?"

"Will it stop us from going to junior high school?" I asked.

Principal Henday's silence told me all I needed to know. I stiffened, waiting for him to lay down our punishment, but then a terrible idea began to rattle around my brain. I hated myself for thinking such a thing, but before I could jam the idea back into its Pandora's Box, it jumped out.

"Remi started it."

My best friend turned around, his eyes wide as saucers and his mouth agape.

The Rake closed my file and opened the other file as he sighed, "Why does this not surprise me?"

"I didn't start it," Remi said. "I swear."

The Rake tapped the file. I tried to convince myself I was getting back at Remi for hiding the news about his other school from me. I tried to tell myself that he deserved this. I had given him enough chances to come clean — to be a real friend.

"Mr. Boudreau, you disappoint me," Mr. Henday said. "I'm surprised we're even having this conversation, considering your father had asked me to write a reference letter for you."

"I didn't start the backpack war," Remi protested.

"Then who did?" The Rake asked.

I waited for my friend to rat me out.

"I don't know who did," Remi said.

Despite what I had done to my friend, he was still protecting me. This was worse than if he did rat me out. My stomach churned and I wanted to come clean, but my mouth stopped working. It was like a bee stinger; once used, it wouldn't work anymore.

"I'm going to have to reconsider writing the reference letter, Mr. Boudreau," The Rake said as he leaned back in his black leather chair.

"But I need it," Remi said. "It's for . . . " His words trailed off.

"Mr. Chan, you'd best leave so I can sort things out with Mr. Boudreau. You can wait outside for your friend."

Remi looked at me square in the eyes. "He's not my friend."

His comment was like a dentist's pick digging into a cavity. No amount of freezing could numb me from the pain of his words. I slunk out the office and into the hallway, looking back once but Remi was facing The Rake.

Trina leaned against the glass of the trophy case across from the main office, waiting for me. For us.

"Where's Remi?"

I couldn't tell her what I had done. I couldn't even look her in the eyes. I wanted to be alone.

"What did The Rake do to you guys?"

I moved down the hallway to get away from her.

"Is it that bad? Is Remi still in the office?" she asked.

I shrugged.

"As long as he keeps quiet, he'll be okay. The Rake has no proof who started the backpack riot," Trina said.

"We should get to class."

"Don't you want to wait for him?"

The door to the principal's office opened and Remi stormed out. As he walked through the main office, he glared at me, then pushed past and headed down the hall to the French section of the school. Trina ran after him and grabbed his arm.

"What happened in there?"

"Ask the monkey butt."

Trina glanced back at me, her eyebrow raised in confusion. I stared at the tiled floor and said nothing.

She asked Remi, "What did The Rake do?"

"I'm done. I'm out. No thanks to you two and your stupid stunt."

"He expelled you? He can't do that."

"Not out of here. I'm out of junior high."

I looked up. Remi looked like a guy who had just found out that Christmas was cancelled forever. I thought this was what I wanted, but now I wished I could take back what I said in the office.

"What's going on?" Trina asked.

"Why did you pin the backpack fight on me?" Remi asked, staring right at me. "You wrecked everything."

"Wrecked what?" I asked. "I don't know what you're talking about."

"That makes two of us," she said.

He explained, "It wasn't for sure, but I was accepted into a sports school in Edmonton. I had to prove I had the marks and I needed a reference letter. My dad asked Principal Henday to write one for me and he said yes, but now he says he's not so sure. He said he didn't want my bad behaviour to reflect on his school's reputation." Remi turned to me. "Great going, Marty."

"Why are you mad at him? He didn't know you were going to the school. Right, Marty?"

I said nothing.

"You knew?" Trina asked, her eyes wide with shock. "How?"

"Does it matter?" I said. "He was going to move away without telling us. What kind of friend is that?"

Trina's gaze narrowed into two angry slits as she started to realize exactly what I had done. She slid away from me as if I had just let out a silent, but deadly, fart. What I had done smelled much worse.

"Don't worry, Remi. I'll prove Mikayla's the cyber bully and tell Principal Henday everything," Trina explained. "He'll know you did this for a good reason and give you the reference letter."

"Too late." Remi turned and walked away.

Trina folded her arms and glared at me.

"Wasn't my fault," I mumbled.

She turned and walked away.

CHAPTER TWELVE

The rest of the morning was a blur. Neither Trina nor Remi would talk to me over lunch hour. When afternoon classes started, I barely heard Ms. Nolan tell us to go to the gym. I just shambled down the hall with the rest of my class. Only when I stepped into the palace of pain and sweat did I suspect something was wrong. Under the basketball hoop, a cart with speakers and a stereo waited for us. It was time for dance lessons.

I joined my classmates on the side while Ms. Nolan checked on the sound system. Remi's blonde-haired teacher, Madame Boddez, led her grade six students into the gym. She was a tank on legs, big and tough and she could run over pretty well anyone. Remi was among the French kids, but he refused to look at me. The two teachers separated us into two groups: boys and girls.

Once we were in our groups, Madame Boddez joined Ms. Nolan in the centre of the gym. Madame Boddez hitched up her sweat pants and scanned the kids. Looking at the teachers and the two lines of students, I thought of flu shot day. No one wanted to go first. Compared to Madame Boddez, my teacher was a ray of sunshine. Maybe it was because the French teacher was so cranky that Ms. Nolan decided to give us a break.

She beamed as she tied her red hair into a pony tail. "Today, you are in for a special treat. You are going to learn a lesson that will serve you well for the rest of your lives."

Madame Boddez was not as positive. "If I catch any of you messing around, you will answer to me first, Principal Henday second, and your parents last. Am I understood?"

A few of the French kids mumbled.

"I said am I understood!" she boomed.

All the French kids shouted, "*Oui*, Madame Boddez."

Even some of the English-speaking students answered in French. Remi's teacher was a cross between a pit bull and a megaphone. She was a hundred times louder than any other teacher and about a thousand times scarier. As everyone stood ramrod straight with their eyes ahead, I knew the teachers were about to pair up the boys with the girls.

Ms. Nolan barked, "Let's start at the far left end. Samantha, step forward."

Madame Boddez yelled, "Far right end. Remi. Go with the girl."

He shuffled out of line and joined Samantha.

"Move it!" the French teacher yelled. "We don't have all day."

As the girls were paired up with the boys, I hoped I'd get paired up with Trina. This would give me a chance to explain everything.

Ms. Nolan called out, "Trina, step forward."

Madame Boddez yelled, "Kennedy, pair up with her."

I felt bad for Trina getting stuck with him, but I knew our teachers' decisions were final.

"Mikayla," said Ms. Nolan.

"Marty," boomed Madame Boddez.

Mikayla flashed a smug smile as I shuffled toward her. We stood side by side, but she inched closer until we were shoulder to shoulder. She smelled of lilacs.

"I'm glad we're paired up," she said.

What was her game? I didn't know why she was so happy about dancing with me. I wondered if she knew we had her flash drive. Maybe she didn't.

"I know why you were trying to take my backpack," she said. Maybe she did.

Ms. Nolan swooped on us. "Marty, pay attention. Hold your hands out like this." She positioned her hands so it looked like she was cradling a frozen turkey.

Madame Boddez barked, "Girls move in to your partner with your arms like so and your head like this."

She stepped up to Ms. Nolan and the two demonstrated how we were supposed to hold our dance partners. The two women looked graceful together, while the students looked more like a cootie outbreak had hit the school and no one wanted to catch the infection.

In front of me, Mikayla smiled as she slipped into my arms. She took my clammy hand and allowed me to put my other hand on the small of her back.

"Now you're going to hear one of the all-time best songs in the world," Ms. Nolan said. "When I was a teenager, this was so cool."

She pulled away from Madame Boddez and pressed play on the stereo. Through the giant speaker, I heard a whiny man sing about being out of love, like it was gasoline for a car, and being lost without his girlfriend. The boys' groans and girls' giggles drowned out the rest of the song. Even Madame Boddez smiled.

"No laughing," barked Ms. Nolan as she put her hands on her hips. We had returned to No Land. "This is Air Supply's finest song."

Madame Boddez clapped her hand over her mouth, stifling what sounded like a laugh.

"Girls, follow the lead of the boys. Boys, slide your left foot forward. Then your right. Now step to the right. Feet together. Right foot back. Left foot back. Feet together. And repeat. Left, together, forward, together, right, together . . . "

On the dance floor, the dancing kids looked like zombies. The jerky movements and the shambling would have been very funny if I wasn't among the dancing dead.

Mikayla looked into my eyes. "LOL. We're F2F at last," she said.

"Uh . . . right." I started to stumble through the steps.

"I thought it was sweet what you did yesterday."

What in the world was she talking about? I decided to play along, hoping to flush out a confession. "What else could I do?"

"I thought I knew what you were up to when you gave me the teddy bear, but when you teased me in the schoolyard this morning, I got confused. Then I saw what you sent last night, and I was like, so OMG."

I pasted on a fake smile, trying to figure out what Mikayla was talking about. Her eyes sparkled as she gazed into mine. We waltzed in silence for a few awkward steps. I stumbled on her feet a few times, but she didn't complain. In fact, her smile was so bright her face practically glowed.

Behind us, Madame Boddez barked, "Nathan Black, this isn't a race. Slow down."

Around us, my zombie classmates shuffled gingerly on crumbling brick feet, barely touching each other. Was this a dance lesson or a horror movie? Mikayla leaned forward and whispered, "By the way, the answer is 'I do'."

The only question that could be answered by "I do" was . . . was . . . no! I shuddered to think of what she was suggesting. I pushed away from her. Ms. Nolan shoved us back together like she was closing the lid of a standing coffin.

"Marty, you have to relax when you're dancing. She won't bite."

Mikayla smiled, flashing her braces at me. Our teacher moved on to another couple.

"Very graceful, Eric. You're a regular, John Travolta," she said as she continued walking among the dancers.

"Who's that?" Eric asked.

"The old guy from that Disney movie," Nathan said.

"I think he's the guy on that dancing show with the old celebrities," Kennedy suggested.

Eric laughed. "You watch a dance show?"

"No way. Not at all. My mom does. It's on when I'm doing my homework."

"That's enough," Ms. Nolan said. "Just keep dancing."

Mikayla moved closer. "Why are you so nervous all of a sudden?"

I stammered, "Uh . . . um . . . uh, you have that kind of effect on me."

She beamed.

I continued, "So, you liked what I sent you last night. I wasn't sure it would get to you so fast."

"Why not?" she inched closer.

"Well, it was pretty big," I said, taking a stab in the dark.

"What?"

"I mean, it was pretty awkward to send."

"You have trouble typing and hitting send?"

Whatever she got must have been an email. "I meant it was hard since I don't have a computer at home. I had to use the library computer and there's always someone watching."

She smiled. "That's so adorable. I can just imagine you sneaking into the library and getting onto one of the stations."

"I wasn't even sure I had the right email address," I said.

Mikayla hesitated. "Why would you need my email address?"

"To send you the . . . the . . . you know."

She broke into a bigger smile. "You mean you sent me something else? I'll have to check my computer after school."

Now I was really puzzled. I had no idea what I had sent her, but it was apparently not to her email account.

"Marty, you should know, though, that I barely check email. Send everything to my friend's account."

"Which friend?"

She laughed and slapped my chest. "You're so funny."

Before I could dig any further, the song came to an end, and the partners broke apart. Ms. Nolan tried to teach us to do something called a line dance as a strange song played about Macarenas, which I thought sounded like macaroons, but the way she was getting us to move, it was more like monkeys. I never had another chance to get close to Mikayla. By the look on her face, she was more disappointed about that than I was.

During afternoon computer lab time, I found Trina huddled beside a computer station with Ida and Samantha. I hoped she had calmed down enough so I could explain myself, but she barely noticed me as I walked up.

"What's going on?" I asked.

Trina ignored me. Ida answered, "We're checking the computer desktop to see if Mikayla might have accidentally saved a file there."

"Listen up," I said. "About the case, there's something you should know."

Trina shook her head, but didn't turn around. Samantha spoke for her. "I don't think Trina wants to talk to you right now."

"But I have a lead."

Now I had their attention. I explained the strange encounter with Mikayla during the dance lesson and hoped that something in the conversation would make sense to one of the girls.

Trina tapped the keyboard as she listened. When I finished my story, she turned to Samantha and Ida. "If Mikayla got something over the computer but it wasn't to her email address, it could only be one thing."

"What?" I asked.

She ignored me. Samantha nodded. Ida motioned Trina to call up the internet browser on the computer. "Load it up. We have to see."

"What are you girls talking about?" I asked.

Trina snuffed at me and tilted her head at Samantha, who turned around to explain. "Mikayla has no real friends, so if you sent something to her friend's account, she wasn't talking about friends with an 's' but Friendz with a 'z.' She's talking about the website, School Friendz."

I smacked my forehead. "Why didn't I see it before? School Friendz!" This was the elementary school version of Facebook, where classmates could post things on their profile or toss virtual erasers at each other or write love notes on the virtual desks. I didn't have a profile on the site, but I had seen Trina's profile a couple of times.

My partner had called up the site and found Mikayla's profile. My mouth dropped open when I saw what was on it. Someone had placed a virtual pink teddy bear on her virtual desk. The bear held a heart that read: M + M 4ever. The sender was me.

"But that's not possible," I protested. "I don't have a Friendz profile. I don't even have a computer."

Ida smirked, "Look what's happening now."

The red heart broke in half to reveal a cartoon couple. The black-haired man in a suit leaned toward the cartoon blonde woman in a red dress and the two kissed.

"Gross!" I shouted.

Samantha laughed along with Ida. Even Trina cracked a smile.

"This makes no sense," I said. "She never liked me before. How could she suddenly like me now just because she thought I gave her a teddy bear?"

Ida shrugged.

Samantha tilted her head, her silver earring dangling from her lobe, "If Marty didn't do this, then who did?"

Trina spoke up. "Hel-*lo*, it's pretty obvious from this that she isn't the cyber bully. Whoever set up the fake profile is the real cyber bully."

"The cyber bully insulted Samantha and me. He didn't try to trick us."

"Not true," Samantha said. "The cyber bully made us think the messages were coming from each other."

"Yes, but the notes were nasty and direct," Ida replied. "This is more like a prank."

"Either way, we have to follow this lead," I said.

Trina nodded. "Someone has to talk to her about the School Friendz posting."

"Who?" I asked.

All three girls turned to me.

For the first time, Trina smiled. "You're going on a date."

Chapter Thirteen

After much prompting, I agreed to track down Mikayla after school and pretend to like-like her so I could get to the bottom of the School Friendz posting. I felt like I was walking into a yard with an angry dog. No matter what I did, I was going to get bit. The best way to protect myself was to catch Mikayla off guard. Unfortunately, she beat me to the punch.

She waited for me by my locker. She clutched her backpack to her chest with one hand and scrubbed her braces with her other hand, taking a whiff of her finger toothbrush. She immediately lowered her hand when she spotted me coming toward her and flashed her braces.

"Just the person I was looking for," I said, forcing a fake smile.

Mikayla giggled. "You were . . . I am . . . oh, this is so going on my blog."

"Can I walk you home?" I asked, holding out my hand to take her backpack.

She handed it over and we walked down the hallway. My shoulder became Velcro, and her shoulder became a woollen sweater. Some of the grade six kids glanced our way and snickered. We strolled past Trina who tugged her ear, signalling that she wouldn't be far behind. I held the door open for her. Before she could step through, Kennedy charged between us, screaming for help as Eric chased him.

"Come back here, beach ball," Eric yelled.

"Help!" Kennedy screamed as he ran around the corner of the school.

"What was that about?" I asked.

Mikayla shrugged, "I think I saw them at recess practising some karate. Kennedy might have gotten a lucky shot just as the bell rang."

"They're such boys," I said.

"Yes, you're much more mature than they are. It's like you're almost a teenager." She brushed her brown hair away from her pale face and looked me over.

"Thanks, Mikayla, but I like to think of myself as more of a . . . a . . . romantic." It was all I could do to keep myself from upchucking from the lame comment.

But the cheesy line melted her heart. If she were chocolate, she'd be a mushy bar right now. The gooey look in her eyes reminded me of the look on the cartoon woman just before she kissed the man. This confirmed one thing for me. Mikayla was no cyber bully, but that didn't mean she wasn't still dangerous. We left the schoolyard and headed down the street. I glanced back. Trina was taking up the rear with Samantha and Ida.

"You know, Mikayla, I'm pretty new at this Friendz website, and I was hoping you could show me how to do some things."

"You're a whiz with the desk postings," she said.

"But what about the private messages?" I asked, fishing for information. "Did they get through?"

"Messages?"

"Um, maybe they didn't get through yet," I said, backtracking.

"You mean there are more love notes coming?" she asked, beaming. She was practically skipping down the sidewalk.

"Maybe I could see your profile," I suggested.

"You'd like to come over to my house?" she asked, breaking into a wider grin.

"Um . . . sure." I glanced back at the girls. They wouldn't be able to help me if I was in Mikayla's bedroom. "Oh, nuts. I can't do it right now. I have to work in my parents' store. Maybe we could stop at the library and you could check to see if my other messages showed up."

"Why don't you tell me what you wrote in the message?" she asked. "That'd be so much more heartfelt."

"I don't think I can remember it," I said.

"Come on, Marty," she said.

"You know what I wrote already."

She stopped in the middle of the street and hefted her backpack on her shoulder. "I'm not budging until you tell me what you wrote in the note. I want to hear it straight from your lips."

I stepped back and waved her off. "Okay, okay, give me a minute. I want to get it right." I glanced back at the girls following us.

Mikayla noticed. "Are you embarrassed to be with me?" she asked, her eyes widening with alarm.

"No, no," I said. "I'm just trying to remember." I scratched at my elbow, signalling Trina that the mission was in trouble.

"I knew it," Mikayla said and stormed away.

Trina waved at me, motioning me to go after her. I shook my head. Trina mouthed the word "now."

Grumbling, I took off after Mikayla and grabbed her arm. She stopped but she glared at me, her mouth looking like an unhappy umbrella about to be flooded with the rainstorm of her tears.

"I'm sorry. I don't know how to explain it, but it's easier for me to express my feelings at the computer than in person."

The rain let up and the umbrella turned upside down. "I know how you feel."

"No, you don't."

"I can prove it." She reached into her backpack and pulled out her flash drive.

"What's on it?"

"Come to my house, and I'll show you."

I glanced back at Trina and the gang, and I realized I had no choice. "Sure."

Mikayla's bedroom was a tribute to all things computer. Over her bedroom wall was a poster of Bill and Melinda Gates. The geeky founder of Windows and his wife stared at me from behind his giant glasses, and I felt like he was judging whether or not I had the right to be in the room. Her bed was neatly made and covered with a pink bedspread. She tossed her backpack on it and grabbed her laptop from the nightstand. She sat on the edge of the bed as she fired up the computer. I wasn't sure where to sit, so I just stood at the doorway looking at Bill Gates.

"Maybe we should do this in the living room or the kitchen," I suggested.

Mikayla smiled. "It's okay. My mom's outside. Enter."

I inched toward her.

She waved me over. "You'll see better here."

I walked to the other side of the bed and stood with my back against the wooden closet door. "Go ahead."

"Okay, I've never shown anyone this before now." She placed the computer on the middle of the bed so I could read the screen:

Shogun Kid
A Novel by Mikayla L. Jackson
Book the First:

In the year 3765, Martin, a young and handsum kid who stood five feet, four inches tall and had black hare and wore silver-framed glasses and was an expert at all things teknologikal, had a majorly serus problem, worse than getting gum stuck in his braces right before a visit to the dentist. He had hacked into the Pentagone's super powerful computer system, and now goverment agents in black suits and dark sunglasses were after his head along with Raven's Eye, the secret evil ajency that hired him to sabotawge the Pentagone computers in the first place. But that wasn't his problem. His reel problem was that he couldn't find her. He had hacked into computers around the entire world to find data about the woman he liked. All he had was a name, Mika. They met on a cyber date (which means they didn't actualy meat in person, but on the internet which is sometimes called cyber space), sending IMs until he reelized that he had to meat her F2F. But the mysteryous woman with the ekaly mysteryous avatar of a black panther dropped off line before he could learn her last name. Now he searched the world wide web for the mysteryous woman he knew that he would evenchaly marry . . . "

She was writing a romantic novel set in some futuristic world. Beside the text was the same kissing cartoon man from the School Friendz heart message that the fake 'me' had sent. I was pretty sure I knew who she had cast as the main character of her novel.

She looked at me, her eyes wide and expecting. I had to say something, but what?

"What do you think?" she asked.

"It's very good," I said. "But I don't understand the line about the 'woman he lived.'"

"That's supposed to be 'loved.'"

I hesitated.

"I really like Martin, don't you?" she asked.

"He's okay."

"He's supposed to be you." She said, batting her eyes.

I wanted to run, but I also knew that I had to see what the cyber bully had sent her. She stood up and walked toward me, cornering me between her closet and the judgmental Bill Gates.

"Will you help me write the ending?" she said.

"Um . . . I don't know the first thing about writing," I said.

"You knew how to write that Friendz note."

"Oh, right, but that was a fluke."

She inched closer, cutting off any escape. "Ms. Nolan said we have to 'write what you know', and you know what's programmed in your heart."

"Ms. Nolan also said you shouldn't use real names in a story."

Mikayla was so close her braces could cut me to shreds if she turned her head slightly. I shifted closer to the poster and knocked into the nightstand, rattling the collection of glass animals on top. A giraffe toppled over. She rushed to the nightstand to protect her zoo.

"Let's bookmark this moment," she said as she righted her collection.

I slipped closer to the doorway, making sure I had an escape route.

She turned around from the nightstand and walked toward me. "Now where were we?"

"You were going to check to see if any of my messages showed up in your School Friendz account."

"Oh, Marty, don't be so shy. Now that we're away from everyone, you can unlock your passion and tell me what's in your heart. Go on."

"Okay . . . I think one of my notes went like this. Mikayla, Mikayla, you're so, so, so, so, very, very, super special."

She shook her head. "That's not like the first note. Tell me again how we belong together like pancakes and blueberries. You made all these delicious food metaphors about your love for me. Tell me more like that."

"Uh, sure. I am the barbecue for you. So, very hot to touch, but smoky and fiery."

"And what am I?"

"The baby octopus tentacles my mom makes. Always clinging on to me."

"What?"

She folded her arms over her chest.

"I mean you're like boiled beef. You fall off the bone with a single touch."

"Are you making fun of me? What's going on here? What happened to the poetry of your first note?"

"I guess I lost it because I'm so nervous. Can we see the first note and that will get me started?"

She eyed me cautiously, then picked up her laptop from the bed and called up her Friendz profile. Over her shoulder, I saw the private message box with a message from the fake 'me'. The note read:

Mikayla, you are the pancake of my life and I hope I can be your blueberry, because together, we'd be so sweet. There are times you make me so hungry to see you again. You're the cinnamon twist that brings a smile to my face, and I want to be the hot chocolate that brings a smile to yours.

She pointed at the screen. "I want more of that poetry, Marty."

"Um, sure, no problem. Give me a second to think."

Ping. The laptop signalled an IM. On the screen, the user name came up as "Marty Chan." The message read: RU there?

Mikayla looked from the screen to me, puzzled. "Are you sending me an IM?"

I shrugged, holding up my empty hands.

Her confusion turned to anger. "Is this some kind of sick joke?"

"No, no, I can explain."

She advanced on me. "You jerk."

"It's not me," Mikayla. "There's this cyber — "

"Get out! Get out of my house right now." She swung at me and connected with my arm. She was surprisingly powerful. I backed through the doorway, rubbing my arm as I went.

"I can't believe I let you preview my story. I hate you. I hate you." She smacked me again and again.

"Mikayla, seriously, that hurts."

"Out!"

I turned tail and ran down the hallway to the living room and blasted out of the front door. Mikayla's mom was mowing the lawn. She waved as I ran past her. I nodded and kept going. A quick glance back and I saw Mikayla glaring at me through the screen door. The look on her face reminded me of the cop shows I had seen, where a killer had just made up his mind to commit murder. I kept running.

Halfway down the block, a shout caused me to skid to a stop.

"Nathan!" Remi shouted into his walkie-talkie. "Come out. We're ready for our first lesson."

A few houses away, my friend stood on a lawn with a couple of grade six boys. Nathan stepped out of the house holding the other walkie-talkie, the one that used to be mine, and he clapped Remi on the shoulder. They looked like they were the best of friends.

CHAPTER FOURTEEN

I crept closer to the house, but stayed behind a parked minivan so Remi couldn't see me.

"Hi-ya!" the boys yelled as Nathan instructed them to practise striking invisible boards. Beside Remi, Eric Johnson machine-gun chopped his "board". On Remi's other side, Ben Winston looked like he was trying to flag down a car with his chopping technique.

Nathan then brought out a real wooden board and waved for his disciples' attention. The minivan provided good cover, but I couldn't hear very well. I moved closer, keeping low and hiding behind a black Camry about a hundred feet away from the action.

"Now I will show you the awesome power of karate. What you see here is a board. I need a volunteer."

Remi raised his hand. "I'm up for anything."

"Very good. Hold this board."

My friend grabbed the board, while the other boys formed a semicircle in front of Nathan. They were eager to see the master in action, and he basked in the glow of their excited gazes. He sized up the board and then yelled, "Hi-ya!"

With one swift move he snapped the thing in half. Nathan was the real deal.

Ben cheered, "Nathan you *pwned* that board. I can't wait until you teach us that. Man, there's a couple of things I'd like to break. Math textbook. My sister's cell phone."

Eric joined in. "I'd chop up the stupid dresser my mom makes me keep my clothes in."

Ben asked, "What's so bad about the dresser?"

"It was my grandma's old dresser and it smells like old lady."

Nathan ignored the ongoing chatter as he walked over to Remi and grabbed the pieces of the board.

"Thanks, Boudreau," he said, patting him on the shoulder.

"You did great, Nathan."

He bowed to Remi, who returned the gesture. Nathan then turned to the group and addressed them: "You guys can learn to do this. My dad is offering karate lessons at a ten-percent discount. Tell him I sent you and he'll sign you up. We can go to the dojo right now."

"Do you think your dad will take an IOU.?" Eric asked. "Because my mom doesn't get paid until the end of the month and I kind of spent all my money on a video game."

Ben inched back. "I thought I was going to get free lessons. You know, because I did your social homework."

Nathan shook his head. "That got you the ten-percent discount."

Eric whined, "But I was hoping to learn some karate *now*, because I wanted to smash in some heads."

"Johnson, you don't use karate to beat people up," Nathan said.

"Then why should I learn it?" Eric asked.

Nathan replied, "You learn it so that people are so scared of you they'll do whatever you want them to do. Once they hear you know karate, Johnson, they'll be shaking in their boots."

Eric quipped, "Maybe I'll tell people I know karate and save myself some money."

Ben laughed. Nathan did not. Neither did Remi, who was now looking in my direction. I ducked low, wondering if he had spotted me. With my back against the car, I noticed why he had turned his head in my direction. Trina, Samantha and Ida were walking toward me. I waved at them to go back. The girls hesitated and then turned around.

"Forget Eric, Nathan. I think karate is pretty cool," Remi said. "I totally get what you're saying."

It was unlike him to suck up. I wondered why he was so chummy with Nathan all of a sudden. I wondered if he decided to get back at me for ratting on him by hanging out with someone else who didn't like me.

Remi made sniffing sounds. "Hey guys, do you smell something?"

Eric asked, "Like popcorn? My mom says I can't eat popcorn. Makes me fart."

He waved him off. "No, it smells more like a rat. And it's getting closer. You guys smell it now?"

Was he talking about Trina? She was already out of earshot.

"I think it's coming from the car," Remi said. "Come out, Marty. I see you."

I started to crawl under the car, but Ben came running around the front. "Spy!"

Remi corrected him. "No, it's a rat. That's what it smelled like earlier."

I scrambled to my feet and backed up, but Eric was behind me.

"What are you doing here, Chan?" Nathan asked. "Alberta's supposed to be a rat-free zone."

Eric added, "Get out of here. Remi told us what you did, slanty eyes."

I ignored his comment, but it was hard to listen to the laughter from the others. It was even harder to see my friend do nothing. Normally, he would have stood up for me. Instead, he turned to Nathan. "Let's get out of here. I can't stand the smell of rats."

"You heard Boudreau, guys. Let's go." Nathan led the group back to his house.

"It's going to be so cool when we get to the sports school, Nathan. I think the first thing we should do is get lockers beside each other."

"Yeah, that'd be awesome. I'll see if my dad can pull some strings with the principal," Nathan said. "They're old army buddies."

Eric interrupted, "How about I do your computer homework and you teach me? You know you need help in computers."

Nathan laughed. "Not from you, Johnson. You're worse than I am. Besides, I've got someone doing my homework already. Listen, the ten-percent discount is good until the end of the week. Drop by the dojo anytime and tell my dad I sent you."

I watched my former friend walk off with his new pals. A burning sensation formed at the pit of my stomach and spread to my chest. My hands curled into fists and my face felt hot, as if someone had slapped me on both cheeks. Something wet streaked down my cheeks, but I wasn't going to wipe it away until Remi and Nathan were far away.

CHAPTER FIFTEEN

Once Nathan and Remi were far down the block, Trina's gang came out from behind the minivan. They rushed toward me, eager to find out what happened in Mikayla's house. That seemed so unimportant to me now, but I brought the girls up to speed.

Trina asked, "And what about what happened here? What was Remi saying?"

I shrugged. "Looks like he's found a new friend."

Ida rolled her eyes. "With that jerk? He's always trying to be better than everyone else. One time, he offered to walk me home. He said he could take care of any enemies, seen and unseen. I told him off."

Samantha smiled, "You're tough, Ida. Good thing you're on our side. Marty, did you get to see Mikayla's Friendz profile?"

I shook my head. "The cyber bully sent an IM while I was in her room. She figured out someone was playing a joke on her, and I'm pretty sure she thinks it's me. It's only a matter of time before she guesses one of you was the accomplice."

Samantha scrunched her face. "Mikayla was our only chance at catching this jerk."

Ida nodded. "You guys have any more leads?"

I shook my head.

"Well, if this is a dead end, then what do we do?" Samantha asked.

Trina was quick to reply. "Give us some time, Samantha. We just have to come up with a new list of suspects. Right, Marty?"

I didn't feel like working on the case any more.

Ida sneered. "I can't believe you losers actually caught me last year. You're terrible detectives."

Samantha nodded. "I could have done better myself."

"We'll find the cyber bully," Trina said. "Give us time. I promise we will figure out a way to catch the cyber bully."

Ida shook her head. "Mikayla isn't going to keep quiet about this. I'll bet she goes to The Rake first thing tomorrow morning to report us. Marty's going to be suspended. Maybe you too, Trina."

My partner looked at me for help, but I had no answer for her. I just walked away.

That night, sleep was like the captain of a dodge ball team picking his line-up. I waited and hoped it would call on next. Only when I was the last player left to be picked, did sleep finally claim me — about twenty seconds before my alarm clock went off. Between worrying about Mikayla telling The Rake, and wondering why Remi became friends with Nathan, I couldn't sleep a wink. I pulled myself from the bed, still unsure about what to do. The only thing I could think of was to throw myself at Mikayla's feet and beg for mercy, like I did when I played dodge ball.

I arrived at school about twenty minutes early. Teachers' cars were parked in the lot, but no students were around. I eyed the east and west entrances to the building, wondering which one Mikayla would use. Eventually, I decided to split the difference and plant myself against the wall between the two.

The weird thing about showing up before everyone else was I got to see how people looked at the start of the day. Some kids were eager to get to school. They were mostly the younger kids who spent much of their classes playing games and learning to raise their hands if they needed to go to the bathroom. Some kids were grumpy; likely they had to write a test or forgot their homework.

Nathan moved through the schoolyard as if he were expecting ninjas to come out from any corner or crevice, or maybe he was just on the lookout for the pesky Kennedy Anderson who wobbled over and handed him a blue binder.

"Now can I get my green belt, Nathan?"

"Not yet, Anderson. Your training isn't done."

"But I did what you told me to do."

"I still have some work that needs doing," Nathan said.

I could care less about Nathan's homework problems. I turned away from the two to see Mikayla. She slipped into the schoolyard from the far end and headed toward the west-end entrance. I moved from my spot and cut her off. She veered away from the building, but I jogged after her.

"Access denied, jerk," she yelled.

"I want to talk," I said.

She clutched her backpack straps and broke into a run.

"Mikayla! Come back."

I chased her to the school shed, away from prying eyes. She finally slowed, trying to catch her breath and adjust her backpack.

"Just hear me out."

"Why? So you can make a fool out of me again?" she said.

"No one wants to make you look like a fool."

"I'll bet you and your friend were laughing over the note. Who was it? Remi, I'll bet. You two twits are always together."

"I can prove that I didn't have anything to do with that School Friendz note, Mikayla. Just don't tell Principal Henday."

She stopped for a second, her eyes narrowing. "Why shouldn't I?"

"I'm not the one who set up the profile. Turning me in isn't going to stop this jerk from doing something else to you. I look guilty right now, but you have to believe me that I didn't send you that note."

"Then why did you want to come to my house?"

"It was part of my investigation. I had no idea you had a crush on me."

She glared at me from behind her glasses. "I do not have a crush on you. I think I *will* talk to Principal Henday."

"If you tell The Rake, everyone's going to know about how you felt."

"How?" she asked.

"I have to tell people some reason why I was suspended from school."

"You wouldn't dare."

I said nothing. It was always best to drop a suggestion and let the other person's imagination turn it into something bigger than it really was. The way Mikayla chewed on her bottom lip, I was pretty sure she had turned my innocent comment into a terrible nightmare of people teasing her.

"But if you hold off, I'll be able to find the real person who did this to you."

She shook her head. "No way."

"I'll leave you out of it, Mikayla. You're not the only victim here. This cyber bully has been pretty busy. What do you say?"

She eyed me up and down. "How can I be sure you're not lying to me now?"

"If I was the one who set things up, why would I want to see the message I had sent? I mean that would make me the dumbest prankster in the world."

This seemed to hit home. She scrunched her face as she tried to make sense of it all.

"Besides, why would I have signalled a partner to send an IM from me while I was still in your house?"

More silence.

"It doesn't make sense, does it?"

She nodded as the truth dawned on her.

"Did the fake 'me' send any more messages after I left?" I asked.

Her eyes widened. "Yes. Last night."

"What did he say?"

Mikayla looked down at the ground and mumbled, "He said if I liked him as much he liked me, I was supposed to wear a pink ribbon in my hair and sing to him at recess."

The cyber bully was devious. Not only would this humiliate her, but it would also put me in the spotlight.

"Did you answer?" I asked.

Mikayla shook her head. "He logged off by the time I came back from chasing you."

"Good. He's expecting you to make a fool of yourself at recess."

"I'm not doing it."

"I have partners who can stake out the schoolyard. We'd know the only person who would be watching is the cyber bully."

She narrowed her eyes. "You're playing me."

"This is the best way to lure out the cyber bully," I argued.

She shook her head. "Lame-oh. I'm not singing in front of everyone."

"You don't have to," I said. "The cyber bully is going to be watching you. All we have to do is spot the person looking at you. The only thing you have to do is walk up to me as slow as you can so my spotters can find the cyber bully."

Mikayla nervously tugged at the bright red ribbon tied around the strap of her backpack. Then she said, "I didn't bring a pink ribbon."

"That red one is close enough."

She let go of the ribbon. "I didn't bring this ribbon because of the note, you know. It's always been there. It's my good luck charm."

"It's okay. You don't have to explain. Now, do we have a deal?"

She nodded.

Later, I found Trina and explained everything. Once she heard the plan, she was up for it. So were Samantha and Ida. The girls would place themselves strategically around the schoolyard to spy on the kids. The person who paid closest attention to Mikayla had to be our cyber bully.

At recess, I rushed to the shed and sat down nearby. I untied my shoelaces and pretended to struggle with a knot. I glanced up to see Trina by the swings. Ida leaned against the wall between the entrances. I couldn't see Samantha, but I was sure she was watching. The chaos of recess fell into its normal routine. Games that were started before school were continuing and kids who couldn't stay awake in class were suddenly alive and running all over the place. Smack dab in the middle of the yard, Nathan was preaching to grade six boys about the power of karate. Among his disciples was Remi. He was helping the chubby Kennedy get to his feet, most likely after a failed karate demonstration. He looked in my direction. I looked away.

I scanned the schoolyard for any sign of gawkers. None so far, but that was because Mikayla hadn't made her entrance yet. I had told her to give my team a few minutes to get into position, but enough time had passed that I worried she had got cold feet.

Finally, the school door opened and she appeared. Her red ribbon now sat atop her head like a lighthouse beacon shining for all the students to see, but no one looked her way. She made a roundabout circuit through the schoolyard, taking her time. I eyed the crowd. Not a single person noticed her. But when she spotted me and started to move closer, one person did straighten up and take notice — Nathan.

As she drew closer, he craned his neck to get a good look. Kennedy and Eric stood in his way as they demanded another karate demonstration. Remi turned and looked my way as well. I stood up to greet Mikayla. Her face was pale and it looked like she was trembling. Her bright red ribbon flopped around like it was electrified.

"Okay, that's far enough," I instructed. "Stay there and get ready like you're going to sing."

She took a deep breath. I glanced over her shoulder and saw Nathan still staring.

"Mikayla, chicken out and head back," I whispered.

She turned on her heel and headed back into the crowd. Nathan grimaced with disappointment. No one else in the group was looking my way. I rushed to gather my team and break the news to them.

Trina shook her head, "Nathan only started looking in your direction after Remi pointed at you."

Samantha glanced across the field at the creepy grade five boy we had all nicknamed Stalker Stan. "He was staring at Mikayla the moment she came out the door and his eyes never left her."

Ida shook her head. "He's in grade five. How would he know any of our account info?"

Trina guessed, "Maybe he's got a brother or sister in our grade."

I shook my head. "It's not the Stalker Stan."

Ida sneered. "Yeah, the guy who just happened to steal your friend is now your prime suspect. You know who I saw looking at Mikayla? Kennedy."

"No way. Kennedy's a wimp," I said. "He'd never bully anyone."

"That guy's scared of his own shadow," Samantha said.

"He tried to ask me to be his girlfriend, but he was so scared I think he wet himself," Ida said. "Definitely not the bully type."

"I'm telling you guys, the cyber bully has to be Nathan."

Trina disagreed. "It's a bit convenient, don't you think? I mean how could Nathan send the IM and teach karate at the same time?"

"He was in the house when Remi and the other guys showed up. He could have sent the IM while they were calling him. I'm telling you, I saw the look on his face when Mikayla walked up to me."

Samantha backed me up. "Well, I did tell the principal about Nathan's nunchuks."

Ida snorted. "No way it's Nathan. The guy was my computer lab partner last week. He can't even turn on the computer, let alone send emails."

"Are you sure about that?" I asked.

"Trust me, that guy might be a schoolyard bully, but he doesn't have the brains to do this," Ida said.

Trina nodded. "Marty, you're letting your feelings about Nathan cloud your judgment."

"I'm sure it's him. There's no way Stalker Stan or Kennedy would have any reason to pick on any of you."

The bell rang to signal the end of recess and our discussion. None of the girls seemed convinced. They turned and headed into the building. Someone crashed into my back, sending me lurching ahead. I barely kept my balance.

Behind me, Kennedy was dusting himself off. Nathan and his cohorts glared at me.

"Watch where you're going, Anderson," Nathan said. "You almost stepped on the rat."

Kennedy protested, "You pushed me."

"Quiet," barked Nathan.

I stood my ground. "I know you did it, Nathan."

"Did what? Take away your only friend?"

"Why are you hanging out with him, Remi? You said he bugged you."

Nathan answered. "Boudreau got tired of hanging out with rats."

"I'm sorry about that, Remi," I said. "I'll make things right. You know I'm getting close to the . . . you know."

"We should go," Remi said to Nathan.

"Yeah, let's go in, guys, and give Chan some alone time so he can cry."

Kennedy and the other guys laughed. Remi gave me a look and shook his head. The boys moved around me. Nathan threw his arm around Remi and walked away.

"Did the plan work?" Mikayla said. She came up next to me.

"Yeah. It's Nathan. I'm sure of it. I just need to get evidence to prove that he's been sending nasty emails to people. Don't worry, I'll leave you out of it. I'm on his cyber bully list too. The emails in my inbox should be enough evidence for The Rake."

"Do you still have the emails?" Mikayla asked.

"Yes, but they came from Ida's email address. The trail would lead to her. We've got to get him to send an email from his own account, except he's probably smart enough to use another fake account."

Mikayla smiled. "I think I might be able to help with your problem."

Chapter Sixteen

Trina and our clients were sceptical about Mikayla's plan, but I told them that this was our only solid lead. Our case was like a buffet table and the only thing left was a dried cantaloupe slice. If we didn't take it, the case would starve. The girls agreed to at least try.

"What we need is for the cyber bully to send me a message," Mikayla said, "And I'll be able to trace it to his computer."

"I have plenty of messages from the jerk," Samantha piped up.

"Me too," Ida said.

Trina shook her head. "I don't think those will work. They came from your email accounts. I'm guessing Mikayla needs one that comes straight from the cyber bully."

"If we had that, we would have caught the cyber bully by now," Ida said, sneering. "The guy is using fake accounts to cover his trail."

"True, but if he sends an IM, there's something you can't fake," Mikayla said. "Every computer has an IP address. It's a postal code for computers, so you can track down their location if you have the right software — which I happen to have."

I explained. "If Mikayla gets an IM from the guy, she can get his IP address and then we go to his house and prove it's Nathan."

"If it is Nathan," Trina corrected. "It might be Stalker Stan or one of the grade six girls for all we know."

"Trust me, it's Nathan," I said.

Samantha flipped her black hair out of her eyes. "What if he sends it from a public computer like the library?"

"What about the school computer?" Ida added.

"Or the internet café uptown," Samantha said.

I waved for silence. "That's why we waited until after school to talk to you. If we get him to send an IM now, we know it can't be from school, which means we've eliminated one of the public places. All we need is someone to stake out the library and the internet café. Any volunteers?"

Ida shrugged. "I'll take the internet café."

Samantha raised her hand. "I'll take the library."

"Great! Trina and I will join Mikayla at her house to send the message. We'll call you if anything comes up."

With that, we split off to our assigned jobs. As we neared Mikayla's house, I couldn't help but glance down the block to see if Remi was at Nathan's house.

"It doesn't make sense," Trina said. "How can a guy who doesn't know anything about computers be so good at hiding his trail?"

"I'll bet he's playing dumb about computers to throw us off the scent," I said.

Mikayla looked down the street. "One thing's for sure, Nathan fits the profile of a bully."

"You know, so does Eric," Trina said.

"Why are you defending Nathan?" I asked.

"Because you only suspected him after Remi started hanging out with him. After what you did, I don't think you have any right to be jealous."

Her comment stung worse than a paper cut on my knuckle. I fell silent as we entered Mikayla's house and took a seat on a black leather couch in the living room. The coffee table was littered with remote controls and old newspapers. She asked us to clear some room for her laptop and left. Trina scooped up the remote controls while I cleared the newspapers. She stacked the remotes on a side table, while I stuffed the papers under the coffee table. The room smelled faintly of disinfectant.

Trina and I plopped on the couch and sank deep into the well-worn butt grooves on the cushions.

"Have you talked to Remi?" I asked.

She nodded. "He asked how you were."

"You told him I was fine, right?" The last thing I wanted Remi to think was that his defection hurt me.

She shrugged. "I didn't get a chance. Kennedy came over and said that Nathan wanted to see him. Remi took off."

"It's weird, isn't it? It's like when Nathan calls, Remi answers. He's become Nathan's lapdog."

She cocked her head to the side, "Yeah, it's weird. I don't see what's so great about Mr. Karate Master, but I'm sure Remi has a reason to hang out with him."

"Maybe he's sniffed out some evidence to prove Nathan's a cyber bully and he's working undercover," I suggested.

"You'd better be careful about your accusations, Marty. If we have the wrong guy, you could get in trouble for spreading rumours."

"I'm not wrong," I said.

She didn't argue with me, but I could tell from her furrowed eyebrows that she didn't agree. I said nothing more, letting the issue rest until I found my proof. Hopefully, Mikayla would provide the evidence. She returned to the living room with her laptop and planted herself between us on the couch. As I watched her load up her Friendz profile, I felt her squeeze her leg against mine. Was she doing this on purpose? If this encouraged her to help us solve the case, I would let her leg stay where it was.

"First, we need Marty's profile," she said. "The fake Marty."

Trina and I leaned forward and looked at the profile. Apparently, the fake 'me' had sent an unhappy face to Mikayla with a note that read: Why didn't you sing?

"Well, we know the cyber bully was in the schoolyard," I said.

Trina nodded. "When did he send this note?"

Mikayla pointed at the time stamp under the note. "About fifteen minutes ago."

"Where's your phone?" Trina asked.

"Kitchen."

Trina got up. "I'll call Ida and Samantha. Maybe they'll be able to see the cyber bully at a computer or something."

"Go for it," I said.

Trina headed off, leaving Mikayla and me alone on the couch. There was an awkward silence.

"Just in case, send the fake 'me' an IM and see if he replies."

"Sure, sure. Good idea." Mikayla put her hands to the keyboard. "What should I write?"

I never thought I'd have to write a love note to myself. "Why don't you tell me, him, you chickened out because I, he, me, whatever, gave you a strange look. Say that your heart is like baking bread. It only rises for him, but any sudden noises — like kids laughing — will make it fall."

"That's so romantic, Marty."

"Uh . . . thanks. Why don't you tell him that if he's really serious about his love, then he should be the one who sings to you?"

Her fingers flew across the keyboard. I'd never seen anyone type as fast as her. I guess it had to do with all the time she spent on the computer. Before I knew it, the message was on its way. All we had to do was sit back and wait. She pressed harder against my thigh. Suddenly, I was very aware of how close we were sitting. I tried to inch away, but I couldn't get out of the butt groove; I just sank in deeper and shifted closer to Mikayla.

"Do you think it will take long for him to reply?" I asked.

"I don't know. Depends if he's on the computer right now."

More awkward silence.

"You think I smell nice?" she asked.

"Um . . . it's okay." I could detect the faint scent of cherries.

She smiled. "It's my mom's perfume. It's pretty fab."

"Say, I wonder what's taking Trina so long," I said.

She shifted on the black leather couch which made a suspicious farting noise as she moved.

"It was the couch," she said, blushing.

I held my breath. Trina rushed into the living room, rescuing me from this awkward situation.

"Ida and Samantha haven't seen anyone from our class at the library or the café. The cyber bully has his own computer."

"We should start making a list of who has computers in grade six," I suggested.

"Hel-*lo*, it would be quicker to make a list of who doesn't have one."

Mikayla agreed with Trina. "Only really poor people don't have computers today."

I looked down at the coffee table. "I don't have a computer."

"Oh. Sorry. I didn't mean anything by it." Mikayla looked at me like I had just told her that I ate cat food for lunch.

Trina interjected. "Remi doesn't have one either."

"Do you think Nathan has one?" I asked.

"If he does, he probably uses it as a door stop," Trina said.

A loud ping from the laptop got all our attention. The fake 'me' responded to our IM with a short note:

Mik, Too shy to sing. Kiss me in class 2morrow, I'll be bacon to your eggs, a delicious breakfast combo. I maxi-mean it. Marty. <33333333.

Mikayla sprang into action, putting her hands on the keyboard and working with great speed and precision. I felt like I was watching a world-class pianist at work. Trina looked over Mikayla's shoulder and nodded impressed.

"It'll take just a few minutes to get the IP address."

Flashing across the screen were a series of alphanumeric strings that made absolutely no sense.

"And you can zero in on the cyber bully's exact location with this program?" I asked.

She continued typing. "No. This gives me the IP address. I have to load another program to get the coordinates of the computer."

"Cool," I said. "Then we'll know for sure *who* the cyber bully is." I nodded at Trina.

She scrunched her freckled face but said nothing.

"It's not that easy," Mikayla explained. "We'll get a roundabout location of the computer. Not an address, but GPS coordinates."

"GP what?" I asked.

"Hel-*lo*, global positioning system," Trina said. "You get the latitude and longitude coordinates so you can pinpoint a location. So you can find people."

I filed away the definition in my memory, remembering that a position could be anywhere on the globe. What a cool system. Except, there was a problem. "How do translate the coordinates into a street address?"

"I'll need a map of Bouvier and a compass. It'll take some time to work out the math and match them up to the grid, but I think I'll be able to figure it out."

"Or, we could just use the GPS in my parents' car," Mikayla suggested.

Trina's face turned bright pink. "If you wanted to do it the easy way," she mumbled.

"What are we waiting for?" I said. "Let's go."

Mikayla climbed out of the butt groove and beckoned us to follow. I sauntered after her. No need to rush. I expected we'd just walk across the street and down the block to Nathan's house. She grabbed a key from the kitchen wall hook, pushed open the back door for us, and led us to the small stucco garage at the back of the house. We had to navigate a landmine of kids' toys from turned-over strollers to various stuffed animals. This looked like a toddler's playground, not the backyard of a grade six student. Trina raised her eyebrow at me. Mikayla caught the look.

"My auntie was visiting with her kids," she explained. "They're not my toys."

She opened the side door and headed inside the garage. I peeked through the doorway at a blue minivan and a carpenter's dream garage. Saws, hammers and workbenches surrounded the vehicle, leaving barely enough room for her to open the driver's door. She reached inside and snapped off a tiny, grey handheld GPS unit that was mounted on the inside of the windshield. Trina and I stepped back as she punched in the coordinates.

"You sure you have the right coordinates?" Trina asked.

Mikayla nodded. "As long as the program gave us the right coordinates, the GPS will lead us straight to the cyber bully."

"Let's move," I said.

Our trio headed into the alley. The small screen revealed a cartoon map of streets and an icon of a car following a green arrow. I knew the cartoon car would end up in front of Nathan's house, but the device barked out "Turn right" in a woman's gruff Australian accent.

"What was that?" Trina asked.

"Voice navigation," Mikayla said, as she ran her finger across the screen. "I'll turn it off. Gets annoying after a while."

More annoying was the fact that we were going in the opposite direction of Nathan's house. Maybe the GPS unit was going to find an alternate route to the house. Instead, the unit led us further away. We were headed toward Main Street.

"Are you sure this thing is working properly?" I asked.

"My parents use it all the time. We never got lost. Well, almost never. One time my dad punched in the wrong address and we ended up in Canmore when we were supposed to go to Calgary."

"Did you enter the right coordinates?"

"I sure hope so," Trina said.

We reached Main Street and turned left. The arrow pointed ahead, leading us along the block and still further from Nathan's house. My heart sank, but little icy ants crawled up and down my legs as we got closer to our target. Even though I was wrong about Nathan, I couldn't help but get excited about the prospect of closing the case. I felt like I was playing a game of chess and I was only one move away from checkmate. All I had to do was wait for my opponent to move his rook so I could capture his king. The win couldn't come soon enough. Halfway down the block, Mikayla came to a stop. The arrow was gone.

"We're here," she announced.

Around us was the liquor store, a convenience outlet, a hair salon and gas station. This was more like a stalemate than a win. There was no way a cyber bully would be sending notes from any of these stores.

Then I noticed it. Across the street, a sign above a shop's picture window caught my eye. It read: Black's Dojo.

I beamed at Trina and Mikayla. "I was right."

Behind the plate-glass window, kids practised karate moves under the instruction of Nathan's father. They threw kicks in the air at invisible opponents and tried to maintain their balance with one foot in the air. They reminded me of my old plastic soldiers that I had to prop against each other because they could never stand upright on their own. Among the wobbly students was Stalker Stan, who was currently trying to work out a charley horse on the sidelines. I imagined Nathan was in the office sending nasty messages on his dad's office computer. I also imagined his reign of terror coming to an abrupt end. I was going to expose him.

But before I could take a step toward the dojo, Mikayla stopped me. "Not like this. We don't want to give him any chance to get away."

Trina nodded. "She's right. If Nathan's at the computer right now and he sees us go in the dojo, he'll know something is up and wipe out the evidence."

"But he's there right now," I said.

"We have to wait until he's out of the office and then we can swoop in like the FBI. Catch him off guard," explained Trina. "So he can't erase anything."

As much as I hated to admit, the girls were right. "Okay, we'll stake out the dojo and wait for him to come out of the back."

"We should get Samantha and Ida," Trina said. "They can help with the stakeout. Plus, they'll want to hear the good news."

"But what if Nathan does something while we're gone?"

Mikayla nodded. "Marty and I can stay here. Together." She moved closer to me. Too close. Way too close.

"You know what?" I said. "Maybe it's better if we get them. Let's go. He's probably going to be here for a while."

Samantha was glad to be relieved of her duties. The town librarian was giving her a dirty look for lurking around the computer stations. Samantha practically skipped out of the building when we came to get her and she broke into a huge smile when I told her what we had discovered. We rushed down the street to tell Ida the good news.

She wasn't so pleased when we found her. She was planted at one of the internet stations at the back of the café, sipping coffee and staring intently at the monitor. The only other users in the café were two old men in plaid shirts who seemed less interested in the computers and more interested in the coffee and conversation with the blonde waitress.

"Good news!" I shouted across the dimly lit café. "We got him."

The waitress shushed us and went back to gabbing with the two men. Our gang navigated the internet tables to get to Ida at the back of the room.

"It's Nathan Black. He's the cyber bully. I was right," I said.

She scowled at me.

"Mikayla traced his message all the way to his dad's dojo," I continued.

Ida shook her head. "It's not Nathan."

"What?" I said.

"Why not?" Trina asked.

Samantha and Mikayla looked at each other, confused.

"Better if you see it with your own eyes," Ida said, waving for us to sit down with her. "This showed up in my email a few minutes ago."

We leaned toward the computer monitor. The still video image of Nathan Black was on the screen. Ida moved the mouse pointer to play the video clip. He looked completely oblivious to the camera as he posed in his karate top and baby-blue pyjama bottoms. He threw punches and kicks at invisible opponents in the middle of what looked like the backyard of his house.

"I see the ninjas of the Green Hand have come to challenge me in my home. In my own home. You will all regret your decision to trespass. Hi-ya!"

Nathan danced around the yard, swinging at saplings and kicking at the air. At one point, he delivered a deadly blow to a little red wagon parked on the lawn. He hopped away, clutching his hand. I had to stifle a giggle, as I watched him dancing around in his teddy bear pyjamas.

"There are too many of you to take with just my bare hands. But I am prepared for you."

He reached behind his back and pulled out a pair of nunchuks. I had seen Bruce Lee use them in old martial-arts movies. The ones in the movies were two black sticks of wood held together with a length of chain, while Nathan's weapons were a couple of rolled-up comic books attached with kite string. He swung his weapon over his head like a propeller, and then brought it down in front of him as if he were striking an invisible opponent. He stepped back and flipped the nunchuks behind his back and under his arm.

Samantha laughed. "He looks like a total loser in those pyjama bottoms."

I shushed her as I watched the video. Nathan went into another series of moves, spinning his homemade nunchuks faster and faster. Behind his back. Under his arms. Around his neck.

Nathan announced, "Now, feel my wrath!"

He flipped the nunchuks off his shoulder and swung them between his legs. He misjudged the distance and the rolled up comic book smacked where the string should have landed. Nathan crumpled to the ground like a frightened armadillo. He yelped in pain and rolled on the grass, his pyjama bottoms slipping down to show off his underwear.

The girls laughed, but Ida shook her head. "Guys, you're not going to like this," she said.

"Why?" I asked.

"The video was sent to everyone in our class."

"So?" Trina said.

Ida looked at me. "Marty sent the video."

CHAPTER SEVENTEEN

Ida replayed the video. Samantha and Mikayla chuckled and pointed at Nathan's bottoms. I felt sick. I was so sure that Nathan was the cyber bully, and now I was staring at proof that he was another one of the cyber bully's many victims. Worse, I was being framed for the video, and I was sure that Nathan was going to want some kind of revenge, and it would involve either my head in a toilet, or the mother of all wedgies. Most likely, a combination of the two along with some purple nurples and snake bites.

Trina patted me on the back, "Okay, it's not Nathan, but we know it has to be someone in the dojo right now. The IM was sent from there so the cyber bully has to be one of the students there."

"Not exactly," Mikayla corrected.

"What do you mean not exactly?" I asked.

"You said the GPS coordinates would give us the exact location," Trina said.

Mikayla shook her head. "Yes, but the IP search program I used might have been off."

"You mean there's a chance that the cyber bully might not be in the dojo?" I said.

Samantha shook her head. "No. It has to be the dojo. The bully is there."

Ida shut down the computer. "Only one way to be sure."

No need to tell me twice. I spun on my heels and led the charge out of the café, down the street. Unfortunately, by the time we got to the dojo, it was empty.

"Maybe we can get a list of the students," Trina suggested.

"Why would Nathan's dad give us that?" Ida said.

"I could talk to Remi," Trina said. "He might help us. I could ask him."

I was pretty sure Remi had made his alliances clear. "No," I said. "Even if he did agree to help, we couldn't get a list of the students before the morning, and by that time Nathan will have heard about the video or seen it."

Samantha patted me on the back. "You can always pretend to be sick."

"Hel-*lo*, Marty won't be able to stay away from school forever. Sooner or later, Nathan's going to get him." Trina turned to me. "What do we do?"

"Let's fan out. Knock on the door of the houses in the area," I said. "Mikayla's search program might have been off by a block or so."

Samantha scratched at her wristband. "It's getting close to dinnertime."

"Lame-oh excuse. I'll help," Mikayla said.

Trina nodded. "Let's go."

Samantha sighed and agreed to go along with the search. We spread out in different directions. I headed behind the dojo and started to knock on doors, but no one answered at the first three houses. Across the street, Mikayla had similar luck.

I pounded on the fourth door and a man in a black jacket answered. The crown and buffalo crest on the jacket meant one thing. I was talking to a cop.

"Excuse me, but I'm wondering if you have a computer in your house," I asked.

"Why do you want to know?"

"Um . . . school project . . . we're doing a survey."

He stroked his bushy brown moustache and unclipped his shirt pocket, pulling out a notepad.

"Really? Who's your teacher? And does she know you're casing houses."

"What?"

"Casing, as in figuring out which ones to rob."

"No, I'm not doing that," I explained.

"Your parents own the Super A Foods, don't they?"

Things were going from bad to worse. "Yeah."

"Tell you what. I've had a long shift, so I'm in no mood for extra paperwork. Go home." He looked across the street at Mikayla. "Tell your friend that I have your name and if anything goes missing from any house on this block tonight or this week, I know where to start looking. Got it?"

I nodded.

"Go."

I hurried off the guy's lawn and grabbed Mikayla. "The search is a bust. Get the other girls and tell them to go home."

"What are you going to do, Marty?"

I shrugged. "I'll figure out something."

This was going to be a long night.

Some people could sense if they were going to have a good day or a bad day just by how they looked when they woke up. If a person jumped out of bed and saw himself in the mirror with perfect hair, he knew things were going to go his way. If the same person crawled out of bed and discovered a giant zit on the end of his nose, he knew his day was doomed. When I woke up the next day, I didn't need to get of bed to know that I looked like dog barf, which Remi often called wet woof. I hadn't slept a wink all night. If I were a slice of pizza, I'd be the one that fell behind the stove and wasn't found for a couple of weeks. I curled up under my blanket and wished I could travel back in time.

"Get up. You be late for school," Mom said.

I peeked from under my blanket. Mom was chewing what looked like a sandwich, but smelled like a pickle jar.

"I'm not feeling good, Mom."

She placed the back of her hand on my forehead. She smelled of pickles and sardines. I suddenly wanted to throw up.

"You not have fever."

"It's my stomach," I lied. "I think I'm going to throw up."

"Maybe you stay home today."

"Yeah, that would be a good idea."

She nodded. "Then you can rub my feet."

"I think I'm starting to feel better."

"I have something stuck in between my toes. You can clean it for me."

I threw my covers off and jumped up. "Must have been a twenty-four-hour flu. I'm good now."

"I think my feet smell bad. You want to check?"

I sprinted out of the room.

In the schoolyard, news of the video had spread. One look at the gawking grade six kids told me all I needed to know. Their gazes followed me as I walked toward the building. I felt like I was in one of those ancient western movies that ran on the oldies movie channel. The kids lined up against the wall and watched me shamble to the shootout. At the far end of the building, Kennedy was showing off something around his waist to Eric and Ben.

"You don't want to mess with me now," Kennedy said.

"Why is it green?" Ben asked.

Eric quipped, "It's because he wiped his snot on it."

"Never disrespect the belt," Kennedy said. "That's the first thing you learn in karate."

There was no sign of Nathan, but I knew he was around. Just like a western movie, the villain gunslinger was always lurking in the shadows. I could stand out in the open and wait for him to pick me off, or I could take cover. I couldn't stand the stares any longer and bolted for the school shed, the only place where I would be safe. My sanctuary from whatever problem I had created for myself. But it was no haven today. Nathan leaned against the wooden doors, waiting for me. He held the black and silver walkie-talkie that once belonged to me.

"I owe you a toonie, over," Nathan said into the walkie-talkie. He clicked it off and lowered the antenna. "Boudreau told me you'd be here."

My friend, my former friend, had betrayed me, but I had no time to think about why he would get payback through Nathan. I had to deal with the bully in front of me. "What do you want?"

"I wanted some alone time with the guy who tried to humiliate me," Nathan said. "Anderson showed me the video. Nice camera work. I don't know when you shot it, but you must have had a good laugh."

"I didn't shoot the video," I said.

"Oh? Who was it?" he asked. "Maybe your girlfriend, Brewster."

"Leave her out of this."

He smiled. "Principal Henday doesn't like cyber bullies in this school. He doesn't like *any* kind of bully. If you want to get off the hook, maybe you should rat out another one of your friends."

"You can't prove that I shot the video," I said. "Besides, I know someone in our class has been using other people's email accounts. There's a real cyber bully and you were just another one of his victims."

He hesitated, "What are you talking about? There are other people getting picked on? Like who?"

"I'm not at liberty to give you that information," I said, "but I have proof that there's a cyber bully in our class."

"Tell me."

I shook my head. "I'm close to finding the culprit. It won't be long before I get him."

"You're bluffing, Chan. If there was a cyber bully, you'd tell me to save your own skin, just like you ratted out your friend. I'm going to the principal."

"No, wait."

"Yes? So what do you know?"

I hesitated. The more people who knew about the bully, the harder it was going to be to track him down.

"I knew it," Nathan said. "I'm going to the principal."

"Give me until lunchtime," I said. "I'll get you proof."

He tilted his head, eyeing me. Finally, he spoke. "Give me a call when you're ready to talk." He tossed me the walkie-talkie.

"I will," I said.

"Noon, or else I go to The Rake." He walked away.

Part of me was relieved that I had some time to catch the real cyber bully, but I was also puzzled why Nathan didn't just turn me in. Maybe he wanted to punish the cyber bully himself. If I was on that video, I know it wouldn't be enough to just see the cyber bully suspended. The really weird thing was how calm Nathan was. Maybe his karate training helped him hide his emotions. The only thing I knew for sure was that his calm and rational threat was much scarier than an angry one.

I headed to the school to find Trina and the other girls. After I told them about Nathan's ultimatum, Trina pulled out a list of names of students. She had been busy.

"Last night, I went through the phone book and looked up all the students who lived within a two-block radius of the dojo. These are our suspects."

The list had three names: Stalker Stan, Eric and Ida.

We all turned to Ida.

She folded her arms over her chest. "You can't be serious."

"She's right," I said. "She was with us yesterday."

Samantha eyed her suspiciously. "Except when she was at the internet café."

Mikayla defended Ida. "But the GPS coordinates for the cyber bully's computer wasn't anywhere near the café."

"Convenient," Trina said. "If I were the cyber bully, this is exactly how I'd get the heat off me. I'd punch in fake coordinates and send people on a wild goose chase."

"Why don't you just come out and accuse me?" Mikayla said.

"Okay, I think you gave us bad information."

Samantha shook her head. "Forget Mikayla. Let's go to the café and check the computer history to see what Ida was doing."

"Not before we check the library computers and see what Samantha was sending."

The lack of leads in the case was pulling the team apart. This was getting us nowhere. I stepped in the middle of the bickering girls.

"I was with Mikayla when the original IM was sent. She can't be two places at once. She's not the cyber bully and neither is anyone else on this team. Okay?"

The girls grumbled, but didn't argue.

"Who's left on the list?" I asked.

Trina held up the list. "Stalker Stan and Eric."

"Eric is no computer whiz," Ida said.

Samantha scratched her head. "And Stalker Stan doesn't know any of us."

Mikayla crossed her arms. "The best suspect was Nathan."

"And we know it can't be him, because now he's a victim," Trina said.

"Plus, he doesn't know the first thing about computers," Ida added.

The bell rang.

As the kids shambled into the building, I turned to the girls. "Let's watch Eric. Trina and I will ask around about Stalker Stan at recess. Maybe we'll stumble onto something."

Trina moved to the door. "But you only have until noon. What can we possibly expect to find out?"

"Just do it, please." I was desperate for any scrap of information. It was like the time I was so hungry in class that I tore off corners from my textbook pages and ate them to silence my growling stomach.

If Eric was the cyber bully, he didn't let on. He seemed more interested in Kennedy's green belt than anything else. In some ways this was the perfect act to throw us off the scent. At lunch, Trina and I stood by her locker and kept an eye on Eric. She opened her locker, pretending to need something, while I watched our suspect over her shoulder. Eric shoved Kennedy back and grabbed his green belt.

"How are you going to keep your pants up now, great karate master?" Eric taunted as he waved the cloth belt in the air.

"Give it back. It's mine."

"Nathan told me I could have the belt, if I could get it from you. Guess what? It's mine now."

"Give it back!" Kennedy leapt up, but he was too short.

Eric laughed and ran toward the entrance with Kennedy puffing after him.

"Give it back or you'll be in big trouble," he wheezed. "Big, big, big trouble. I maxi-mean it."

Trina and I turned to each other at the same time. Our mouths dropped open. We bolted after Kennedy and caught him halfway across the parking lot. We each took an arm and hustled him toward the shed. Eric was long gone with the green belt, using it as a guitar for a rock band performance to impress the nearby girls.

"Let go of me," whined Kennedy.

"Not until we've had a little talk," Trina said.

"You're hurting me."

I gripped his arm harder. "That's the least of your worries. We know about the video."

"Yeah, everyone does," he wheezed. "You're the one who sent it."

"No, you did," Trina accused.

He stammered. "Wha . . . wha . . . what are you talking about? I'm Nathan's best friend. I'd never do anything to him. Why would you even say that?"

"Cut the act," I said. "We know you've been sending notes to Samantha, Ida and Mikayla. It's over, Kennedy."

"You guys are crazy," he said. "Why would I send anything to a bunch of girls?"

"That's what we want to know," Trina said. "The sooner you talk, the easier things will go for you."

"Help," he squealed. "Help!"

"Let him go," Remi said, coming up from behind.

"Remi, leave us alone. We have a break in the case," I said.

"Drop him," he ordered.

We did.

"You okay, Kennedy?"

The pudgy boy rubbed his arms with both hands and glared at us as he ran behind Remi. Trina took a step after him, but Remi blocked the way.

"Why are you protecting him?" she asked.

"Nathan said he saw you guys grab Kennedy. He didn't want his karate student to be hurt, so he sent me as protection."

"Hel-*lo*, you're protecting the cyber bully," Trina said.

"Let us do our job," I said. "Go play with your new friend."

"Can't do that. Nathan's waiting for us, Kennedy." Remi ushered the boy toward the school.

"When did you become Nathan's errand boy?" I said.

Remi shot back. "You wouldn't understand. Let's go, Kennedy."

Trina shook her head. "He's going to erase his tracks as soon as he gets near a computer."

"Let's make sure he doesn't," I said.

We headed to the school computer lab, but the door was locked. The school library was the only other place Kennedy could find a computer. But as we rushed down the hallway to the library, we passed Trina's locker. I skidded to a stop when I noticed it was open. Hanging out of the locker was a white paw. I motioned her to stop. She opened the door and the Stuffy Spy fell to the floor.

"What's this doing here?" I asked.

"I don't know," Trina said.

Before I could hazard a guess, there was a tap on my shoulder. Nathan and a group of grade six students stood behind us. "It's noon, Chan."

"I need more time."

"Hey, what's that teddy bear for?"

"Hel-*lo*. None of your business," Trina said.

"Oh, I think it is my business," Nathan said. "Remi said you guys had some kind of spy equipment that looked like a teddy bear."

I was no longer the only rat in the school.

"Let me see the stuffy," Nathan said.

Trina shouted, "No way."

"Back off," I warned.

He advanced as more kids gathered around us. Nathan snatched the white bear out of Trina's hands and examined it from head to butt. He found the flash drive. "I knew it. This is what you used to record that video of me."

The kids muttered to each other.

Nathan waved for silence. "I'm sure Principal Henday would be very curious to see what's on this thing. Don't you think, guys?"

The crowd cheered. Behind the kids, Remi and Kennedy approached. I shot a laser-beam stare at Kennedy. The strange thing was that he shrank away from my glare and hid behind Remi. The round kid had to be the cyber bully, because he was a computer whiz and he used the word "maxi-mean". The only thing that didn't make sense was that he wasn't a bully at school. He was more of a follower. Plus, for a guy who was about to successfully frame Trina and me for his crime, he wasn't acting like he had just beaten us. Instead, he looked scared.

Trina leaned toward me and whispered. "How did Kennedy plant the Stuffy Spy in my locker when we were with him? He can't be in two places at once."

The truth smacked me square between the eyes. "Trina, he can't be in two places at once, but the cyber bully can."

She raised her eyebrow, confused.

I tapped Nathan on the back. "I'm tired of you pushing me around."

He turned around, squeezing the Stuffy Spy by the neck.

Trina whispered, "Are you trying to get killed?"

I ignored her. "Everyone's scared of Nathan because they think he can beat them up with his karate, but the truth is, I've never seen him actually do anything other than break a board. And who's to say the board wasn't already broken."

He seethed, sucking air between his gritted teeth. "Take that back, Chan."

"What are you going to do? Get one of your flunkies to bully me over the internet?"

He hesitated. "What's that supposed to mean?"

I glanced at Kennedy. His lip started to quiver. I had to keep pushing. "I'm not one of your lackeys, Nathan. I'm not going to do anything you say just because you threaten me or offer me a green belt."

"Shut up, Chan if you know what's good for you."

I shook my head. "Or else what? I don't think you even know karate. All show and no action."

Trina tugged on my sleeve to stop. I moved away. By now, almost all the grade six students had gathered in the hallway along with a few of the younger kids.

"You're the faker," Nathan spat. "You don't even know your own culture."

"Hey, man, take it outside," Remi said. "Teachers are going to notice."

"What do you think we're going to do outside?" I asked. "Get another lackey to do your dirty work."

"You know what?" Nathan said. "I've always wanted to prove that karate was better than kung fu."

Eric blurted, "Fight."

The word "fight" rippled through the crowd as if a large stone had been dropped in a pond. It definitely made waves with the murmuring kids.

"After you," I said.

Nathan scanned the eager faces of the other students and headed out. I kept an eye on Kennedy, who shrank back from Nathan. The pudgy boy was the key to the entire case, and I had to get him to confess.

We headed to the shed for the faceoff. The students formed a circle around Nathan and me. Trina chewed on the end of her hair. Mikayla shifted from one foot to the other. Ida and Samantha shook their heads, but I forced myself to look away from them. I focussed my attention on Kennedy, who was now hiding behind Eric and Remi.

Nathan stepped in front of me and rolled up his sleeves. "This is going to be so sweet."

"You sure you want to get your hands dirty, Nathan?"

"You should be more worried about your own hands."

"I doubt you have the guts," I taunted. "You know The Rake's policy about fighting. You could be suspended."

He hesitated. Definitely a weak spot.

I took a stab in the dark. "Maybe that's why you moved to our school this year. You were caught fighting at your last school."

"Shut up. You don't know what happened at my last school."

"Make me shut up, Nathan," I said. I was really hoping he was lying all this time about being a karate expert. I was a bloody nose away from finding out the truth.

He wound up, and then stopped himself. "You know what? You're right. You're not worth it," he said.

Disappointed groans trickled through the crowd.

He waved at the crowd for silence. "Shut up. I didn't say there wasn't going to be a fight. I have a better idea. Boudreau, you do it," he ordered.

"What?" Remi looked as shocked as I felt.

"You want to get in the sports school, don't you? Well, you're not getting in without the reference letter from my dad. You do this, and I'll make sure he writes it for you. Then you'll be in just like that." Nathan snapped his fingers.

My former friend gaped at me and rubbed his thighs, unsure of what to do.

"If you don't beat up Chan, you stay in Bouvier next year. Goodbye hockey school. Goodbye NHL dreams."

Remi took a deep breath. "Okay, I'll do it."

The crowd cheered as he advanced.

Chapter Eighteen

"Hold on, hold on," I said. "Give me a chance to warm up."

Remi stepped back, giving me enough space. I closed my eyes tight and did some deep breathing. In. Out. In. Out. In. Out. In, out, in, out, in out. I started to get dizzy and stopped. Then I opened my eyes and threw a couple of practice punches in the air. The kids snickered as my spaghetti arms flailed around the air. I unleashed a kick in the air and planted myself in a wide stance just as I saw Jackie Chan do in his movies.

Riiiiiiiiiipppppp. My pants split right up the butt, leaving my baby blue underwear completely visible to all the kids behind me. The girls squealed. The boys laughed. Even Remi smiled.

"Enough fooling around," Nathan yelled. "It's time."

Eric started a chant, "Fight, fight, fight."

Ben picked it up, "Fight, fight, fight."

Kennedy looked down at the ground as the rest of the kids quickly joined in. "Fight, Fight, Fight!"

Remi put his fingers in his mouth and let out a sharp whistle, which quieted the crowd. He stepped forward and raised his hands. The most popular kid in grade six, and star hockey player of the Bouvier Bobcats, was about to pound on me. He cracked his head to the side a couple of times and prowled around me.

Nathan ordered, "Kick his yellow butt. Give him what he deserves."

I backed away from Remi. "Don't do this. This is between Nathan and me."

"Let's see some action. Fight!," Eric yelled.

Trina shouted. "Keep quiet, Eric. I'm getting the principal."

"Stop her," yelled Nathan.

Eric cut her off, but she shoved him aside. Ben Winston and a couple of other boys jumped in to keep her from leaving. She put up a good fight. Mikayla tried to make a move, but Stalker Stan squawked, "Someone else is trying to leave."

Nathan yelled, "Grab her. No one leaves."

Kids crushed in, hemming in my partners and blocking off any escape. I couldn't see Trina any more. I hoped she was able to get away, but I didn't have time to worry about her now. Remi charged at me. He took a swing, but he didn't put much effort into it. I ducked the blow and stepped away.

"You call that a punch," Nathan said. "I told you to beat him up."

The kids cheered.

Remi straightened up and faced off against me again. He swung at my head. I ducked. Swish. The punch didn't even connect.

Nathan yelled, "Boudreau, kick his butt!"

Remi charged at me. I ran out of the way. The kids booed. Apparently, running was not an acceptable fighting tactic, but it bought me time.

"You know this is stupid. Nathan's making you beat me up because of a video that he claims I made, but I know who really did it." I turned to Kennedy, who looked like he was going to hurl.

Nathan ordered, "Boudreau, this is your last chance. Hit Chan or forget the sports school."

Remi glared at Nathan and turned toward me, curling and uncurling his fists. He looked like he had been asked to put down his dog. Until this moment, I didn't know how much the sports school had meant to my friend. The opportunity was within his grasp but I had snatched it away. I was the one who drove him to become Nathan's lackey. I was the one who created this mess. I was the one who ruined my friend's dreams and there was only one way to give them back. I lowered my hands.

"Hit me," I said.

He shook his head.

"Hit him!" Nathan barked.

Remi lowered his hands.

"I deserve this for what I did. Please. It's okay. Do it."

The kids roared encouragement.

I closed my eyes and waited.

Nothing.

I opened my eyes. Remi was still standing there.

"I can't hit you," he said.

"Why not?"

"Your mom'll get mad if you break your glasses and she might make you clean her toe gunk again."

The crowd let out a collective "ewwww."

I took off my glasses and stepped within Remi's reach. Without my glasses, the world dissolved into a great big blur. "Go ahead."

"You might get blood on your shirt."

"Do it!"

"NO!"

I kicked him. Hard, in the shin.

The crowd let out a loud "ooo."

"Ow! What did you do that for?"

"So you'll hit me."

"Well that's kind of stupid. Now I do have to hit you."

"Finally." Nathan said, nearly drowned out by the impatient kids whose "ooo's" now turned to "boos."

I closed my eyes.

"Open your eyes, Marty. I don't hit guys in the back or people who close their eyes. It's got to be fair."

"Fair is Nathan doing his own dirty work," I said. "But he's too much of a chicken to do that."

Nathan yelled. "You want the letter or not, Boudreau? Just do this one last thing. It's not that hard."

My eyes popped wide open. There was Nathan's fatal flaw and my opening. "He'll never hold up his end of the deal, Remi. He makes promises he'll never keep. Isn't that right, Kennedy?" I turned and squinted toward the general area where I thought he was standing.

"Um, he's over there," Remi said as he nudged me a few degrees to the right.

"Tell everyone what Nathan made you do," I said as I put my glasses back on.

"Keep your mouth shut, Anderson," Nathan barked.

Kennedy seemed to shrivel in the crowd.

"I saw you begging Nathan to teach you karate, but he never did teach you, did he? All he did was take a belt from his dad's dojo and give it to you. It wasn't even a black belt. I bet he said you had to earn the black belt with more favours, right?"

Kennedy glared at Nathan, but said nothing. Instead, my words seemed to have an effect on my friend.

Remi turned to the karate master. "You were never going to get me the reference letter, were you?"

"I'll keep my promise this time, Boudreau."

"Be honest," I said.

"Shut up, Chan!"

"Don't talk to my friend like that," Remi defended me.

"That's how it's going to be, eh Boudreau. Okay, well it doesn't matter. Chan's still on the hook for the video he shot."

"I didn't send it," I said.

"It came from your email address," Nathan said.

"Someone hacked into my account."

He laughed. "Leaves me out. I can't even get into my own email."

I smiled. "Yeah, I know, and so will The Rake when he investigates. If you're in the clear, who do you think The Rake will go after for the video? Especially after I show him the messages that were sent to me, Samantha, and Ida. He's going to figure out the same person is behind the emails and the video. Who do you think that's going to be?"

"It ain't going to be me, Chan."

I turned to Kennedy. "It's going to lead to you."

He stiffened, his eyes wide with fear.

"And do you know what The Rake will do?"

Remi turned to the quivering boy. "I bet it'll be three strikes all in one. Maybe the cyber bully will get suspended or even expelled."

Kennedy looked like he was going to burst into tears.

Nathan laughed. "The kid's not going to help you, Chan"

"And I'm pretty sure Nathan isn't going to help you, Kennedy. All that grief for a green belt," I said. "Was it worth it?"

The crowd fell silent as Kennedy glanced from me to Nathan, wrestling with his fear, guilt, and anger. His face contorted into a grimace and his right eye developed a weird tic. Finally, he turned to the other kids.

"Forget that!" he blurted. "Nathan came up with — "

"Don't you say another thing or else you'll never get the black belt," Nathan warned.

Remi cut him off. "You'll never get the black belt, Kennedy. At least not from him."

"They don't know what they're talking about. I gave you a green belt. You have to earn the black belt. And that means shutting your fat mouth right now."

"I'm not sure he even knows karate," I said. "The video proves that much."

"I was messing around," Nathan yelled.

Kennedy turned to the crowd. "He made me do it. He made me shoot the video and send it from Marty's email account. Marty, he wanted to frame you when he learned you were trying to track down the cyber bully."

"You fat piece of lard. You're the one who knows about people's passwords. I can't even start a computer."

"You said you'd teach me karate if I helped you get revenge on Samantha for snitching on you about the nunchuks you brought to school."

"No way, fatty. You were the one who wanted to get back at Ida because she turned you down when you asked her out."

Some of the boys chuckled.

Kennedy's face turned bright pink. "Nathan told me he got kicked out of his last school for bullying. He was making me send the messages so he wouldn't get in trouble here."

"Shut up, tubbo!" Nathan screamed.

He pushed Kennedy down. I jumped in front of Nathan, but he shoved me to the ground as well.

"Chan's trying to frame me," Nathan explained to the kids.

"I know you did it, Nathan," I said.

"You sent that embarrassing video of me, and the evidence is going to point to you and Trina. The teddy bear spy was in your girlfriend's locker."

Kennedy replied, "Nathan probably planted the teddy bear in Trina's locker to frame her."

"I never heard of the Stuffy Spy," Nathan said.

"Liar," I accused. "You said Remi told you about it."

Remi shook his head. "I didn't tell him anything. The only way he could know about it is if he stole it from us."

Nathan fell silent, but Kennedy wasn't done talking. "Nathan made me send the video from his dad's dojo. The evidence is on the computer. Go and check."

"You are dead, fat boy!"

"I don't think so," boomed The Rake. He stood at the back of the crowd with Trina. The kids parted like the Red Sea for Moses as he approached Nathan. "Mr. Black. Mr. Anderson. My office!"

The Rake led the boys away. The kids converged on each other after they left and chattered about what had just happened. Ida and Samantha ran up to Trina and me and slapped our backs in congratulations.

Mikayla walked up and gave me a peck on the cheek. "Thank you for not telling everyone about what Nathan did to me. You're just like the Shogun Kid in my novel, but so much nobler. And cuter, too."

I blushed. "Um, thanks. Can you excuse me for a second?"

I moved away from the adoring Mikayla and headed to Remi who stood off to the side, looking out of place during the celebration. He smiled when he saw me.

"Were you really willing to let me hit you?" he asked.

"If it meant you could get into the sports school, yes."

Remi shook his head. "You're nuts."

I nodded. "I'm sorry I ratted you out. It's just that I didn't want . . . well, I didn't want you to . . . it's complicated. Anyway, I'm sorry."

He clapped his hand on my shoulder. "Yeah, I know."

"I'll talk to The Rake and tell him I started the backpack fight."

"You could get suspended for it," he said.

"If it gets you in the sports school, it's worth it."

He cracked a giant grin and punched me in the arm. I smiled back.

Nathan and Kennedy were suspended from school. Kennedy got one week, while Nathan was out for two weeks at least. Rumour had it that he had to see a counsellor to deal with his anger issues and once he was cleared he could come back. Mikayla said she heard Nathan's parents yelling at him for three straight nights. She thought she might have also heard Nathan crying, but she couldn't be sure.

A few days after the incident, Principal Henday gave a lecture at a special school assembly about cyber bullying. As the kids listened in the gym, I saw a lot of kids nodding. They might not have been Nathan's and Kennedy's victims, but they were victims of some kind of cyber bully. After the lecture, I told Mr. Henday about the backpack fight and why I started it. Instead of a suspension, he gave me one week's detention.

"That's because you flushed out the cyber bully," he said. "But next time, report it to me and let me take care of it."

"Yes, sir. What about Remi's reference letter? Will you write it for him now?"

"Already done. It's on its way to the junior high school principal," Principal Henday said. "I just hope Remi remembers that when he gets to the NHL."

"Thanks, Mr. Henday."

"No more trouble, Marty. At least not until you graduate. Deal?" He held out his hand to shake. I grabbed it and sealed the deal.

It was official. Remi was going to go to a different school next year. Things were going to change between us. For some reason, that thought didn't make me feel that bad any more. I served my first day's detention and then headed to the store, fully expecting Dad to yell at me and Mom to make me rub her feet. Instead, I found Remi and Trina outside the store.

"Took you long enough," Trina joked.

"Take it easy on the guy," Remi said. "He's probably going to get an earful once he gets in the store."

"Congratulations, Remi," I said. "The Rake told me you're going to get in the school."

"Yeah, thanks to you."

Trina said, "I guess that means we won't be seeing that much of you next year."

"I'll come back for visits," he said. "Someone has to protect Marty from you."

"Hel-*lo*, you'd be crying for your mommy."

Remi laughed.

"Maybe we can go out and see your hockey games," I said.

He nodded. "I'll send you the schedule. But if you can't get to Edmonton, it's okay too."

"We'll be there," I said.

"I'm just saying I'd understand if I didn't see you at all the games."

Trina sighed. "No point in worrying about next year. We still have some of this school year left. Who knows? Maybe we'll have another case to solve before the summer. You guys up for another one?"

"Yeah," Remi and I said at the same time. "Jinx."

"Double jinx," Trina said. She punched us both in the arm.

"Ow," I said.

"Good shot."

"See you boys tomorrow," she said. She walked away.

Remi stayed back. "Need help in the store?"

"My mom might have a new job for you," I said.

"What is it?"

"She needs someone to rub her feet."

He scrunched his face like he had sucked a lime. "No way. You're on your own, Marty."

We laughed until a rap on the store window got our attention. Mom was standing on the other side. She lifted her foot and pointed to it with her pickle.

Remi gasped. "Gross. I thought you were kidding. So nasty."

"I should get going," I said.

"Sure. Hey, Marty, you might want this." Remi reached in his pockets and pulled out his walkie-talkie. "You can have mine. For the next case."

I smiled and reached in to my pocket to pull out my walkie-talkie. "I have mine. You keep yours so we can stay in touch."

"Um, the range isn't . . . " he started.

"It'll give us a reason to get together."

Remi smiled. "Okay."

He put his walkie-talkie back in his pocket and walked away. I looked at the walkie-talkie in my hand and pictured my best friend at the other end. I wouldn't know what he was saying, but I didn't care. I just liked the idea that he would always be at the other end.

Suddenly, the walkie-talkie squawked to life. "Momma Bear, come in. Over."

I smiled and pressed the talk button. "Yes, Alph . . . Baby Bear, I hear you. Over."

"Do you really have to rub your mom's feet? Over."

"Unfortunately, yes, I do. Over."

"Gross. See you tomorrow? Over."

"Definitely," I said. "Over."

MARTY CHAN is a nationally-known dramatist, screenwriter, and author. His juvenile novel, *The Mystery of the Frozen Brains*, won the Edmonton Book Prize, and was also listed as one of the Best Books of 2004 for grades three to six by *Resource Links* magazine. The second book in the Chan Mystery Series, *The Mystery of the Graffiti Ghoul*, was shortlisted for the 2007 SYRCA Young Readers' Choice Diamond Willow Award, the 2007 Golden Eagle Children's Choice Book Award, and the 2007 Arthur Ellis Crime Writers of Canada Award in the Best Juvenile category. Marty Chan lives in Edmonton, Alberta.